Wahida Clark Presents Publishing
60 Evergreen Place
Suite 904A
East Orange, New Jersey 07018
973-678-9982
www.wclarkpublishing.com

Copyright 2014 © by Kayenne

Library of Congress Cataloging-In-Publication Data:
Kayenne
SWIPE
ISBN 13-digit 978-1936649-59-4 (paper)
ISBN e-book 978-1-936649-10-5
LCCN: 2014916250

1. New Orleans-   3. Credit Card Fraud-   4. African American-Fiction- 5. Urban Fiction- 6. Street

Cover design and layout by Nuance Art, LLC
Book design by NuanceArt@aCreativeNuance.com
Edited by Linda Wilson
Proofreader Rosalind Hamilton
Printed in USA

SWIPE

BY

KAYENNE

SWIPE

KAYENNE

ACKNOWLEDGMENTS

I want to thank all of the readers for reading my latest creation. I hope you enjoy Trina, Mia, and China's story.

Kayenne

SWIPE

KAYENNE

CHAPTER ONE
Katrina "Trina" Bell

Bam! Bam!

A short red-bone wearing a faded purple house coat and purple scarf around her head knocked on Ray Ray's SUV window a few seconds after he pulled up in my driveway.

"Chill out. Let me handle this," Ray Ray said to me as sweat dripped from his forehead.

"Screw that." I brushed my long micro-braids out of my blemished free face and jumped out of the passenger seat, placing the two hundred dollars Ray Ray had just given me into my bra.

Before Ray Ray could react, I was standing outside on the driver's side facing the petite woman with watery brown eyes. She folded her arms and bit down on her bottom lip and tapped her dingy white house shoe against the pavement.

"Who the fuck are you?" I asked.

"I-I-I'm his wife," she stuttered.

"Wife? He's been with me for the last six months." I couldn't help but feel played. I should have known something wasn't right on those days he would disappear. Ray Ray worked in the oil field, so it wasn't unusual for guys to be gone days at a time. Little did I know that he was only at his wife's house pretending to be off somewhere working.

SWIPE

Ray Ray's wife looked me up and down. She took in my cocoa brown, round face and my pink top and tight jeans. Mrs. Redbone uncrossed her arms. I saw her eyes dim when she realized that physically she didn't match up. I was thick in all the right places. She was a little on the slender side. Compared to me, she was flat in the front and the back. My small waist only brought attention to my big ghetto booty, an asset I wasn't afraid to flaunt and she couldn't help but notice it.

Ray Ray's sorry behind remained sitting behind the wheel with his head in his hand.

"We just celebrated our third anniversary," Mrs. Redbone said as her voice cracked and tears flowed down her cheeks.

"What that got to do with me?" I shook my head in disbelief.

"I'm just trying to get you to understand why I'm here," she responded.

"That's between y'all. I ain't got nothing to do with it."

"What do I have to do to get you to leave him alone?" she asked.

"Excuse me?" I responded.

"Do you want money? I'll write you out a check now."

"Are you serious?" I couldn't believe this chick. She was beyond thirsty. Besides, I'd just gotten a few hundred from Ray Ray. Not enough to cover rent, but I wasn't about to accept nothing from this crazy heifer. If I took the check, she would probably claim I stole it and forged her signature.

KAYENNE

"How much is your rent? Four hundred . . . five hundred a month?" She looked up at me with contempt in her eyes.

Ignoring her question, I asked in a calm voice, "What's your name?"

"Felicia Rochelle Williams." She emphasized the word Williams.

"Well, Felicia, I'm Katrina and I ain't got time for this shit. Ray Ray is all yours."

I pulled the door open while Ray Ray unsuccessfully attempted to lock it. His eyes widened when he looked up at me and saw the anger in my face.

"Ray Ray, get your sorry ass out that truck and get your shit out of my house!" I yelled as I hit Ray Ray on his side with my free hand.

I walked past his wife and into my quaint two-bedroom rented house straight to my bedroom.

Ray Ray followed. Not sure of what he was going to do, I went to my closet and pulled out my gun. He backed up when I started waving it in his direction.

"Trina, you've lost your mind. Put that gun down."

"Your wife is waiting for you outside, so I suggest you hurry up and pack your shit."

"Wife . . . what you talking about? That's some random 'ho who's mad because I'm with you and not her."

"Stop with the lies. Now get your shit and get the fuck out of my house, or do you want me to call the Shreveport PD to get you out?" Ray Ray had some warrants, so I knew mentioning the police would

9

make him act right. I aimed the gun directly at his balls.

"Trina, come on now, you're making me nervous with that gun."

"I suggest you get to moving, and you wouldn't have to worry about my gun."

Ray Ray continued to protest, but he moved his fine, muscular self around and threw some of his stuff in a duffle bag he'd kept under his side of the bed.

"I'll be back." Ray Ray attempted to kiss me, but I blocked him with the end of the gun.

He pushed me away. "You crazy."

"You having your wife come to my house with all this drama is crazy." I walked him to the door.

"Come on, girl. I don't love her. I love you."

"Fuck love."

I opened the front door. Felicia turned when she heard the door open. I pulled one of Ray Ray's muscular arms and pushed him out. "Here's your husband. Now get off my porch!"

Once Ray Ray was out of the house, I shut my door and locked it. I could hear them going at it as they walked away. I looked out my window and saw Felicia constantly hitting Ray Ray on the arm. He held on to her and she eventually stopped. I don't know what he said to her, but she walked to her car and he got into his SUV. They both backed up and drove off.

Poor Felicia Rochelle Williams, I thought as I went back to the room and put up my gun. I reached inside my bra to take out the money. *Bribing me to stay away from her husband.* All I removed was a twenty dollar bill. *But where's the rest?* I wondered, frantically patting and checking my bra. Anxious, I began retracing my steps. Then I grabbed my cell phone to call Ray Ray, but a text from him was already waiting.

The money fell and yeah I got it. You pulled a gun out on a brother. Twenty is better than nothing. But you know what to do to get the rest back.

I released a 'getting tired of Ray Ray's ass anyway' sigh, but I sure would miss how he laid the pipe and his money. I had two weeks to supplement the money I was getting from him because rent would be due again. My little job at the fast food restaurant only covered my utilities. Plus, it was almost time to get my nails and braids re-done. I needed to find a replacement-man and soon.

SWIPE

CHAPTER TWO
Mia Jackson

"Mia, please. I know you just sent me a money order, but can you put fifty more dollars on my books? I promise you that's all I'll need to get me through the month," Tony Jackson, my incarcerated husband, begged from the other end of the phone.

I rolled my eyes. *Why does he need all of that money behind bars?* He had more money on his books than I carried in my Michael Kors purse at any given time. Between the collect phone calls and his constantly begging for money, I would never be able to make ends meet.

"You know I love you, right?" Tony said.

"Of course you do. Who else would put up with your shit for this long?" I responded.

"Stop it, girl. We ain't got much time left on this call. Tell me you love me."

Tony knew I loved him, but right now as I glanced at my checking account online while talking to him, I could only think about my dwindling bank account.

"Say it," he said again.

An automated voice said, "You have one more minute left on this call."

"Okay, Tony. I love you too. Satisfied?"

"I know you do. You're my ride or die chick."

KAYENNE

"Yeah. Yeah. Check your books in about three days."

"Overnight it . . ."

The phone clicked. The call ended. I placed the phone on the nightstand by my bed.

"Mia, come on, girl. Get off that computer and let's get back to what we were doing before we got interrupted by that phone call," Casper said. When standing, Casper was barely 5-feet 4-inches tall. I towered over him by two inches without heels on. What Casper lacked in height, he made up for in length. His thick dick kept me satisfied on many nights.

I know I'm married, but I'm only twenty-three years old and I have needs. With an hourglass shape and pretty face, finding men to take care of those needs wasn't a problem. With Tony locked up in a Louisiana penitentiary for ten years on drug charges, I needed a maintenance man because there's some things a sex toy just couldn't replace.

Not sure of how much longer I would be dealing with Casper, I decided to get one last romp before giving him his walking papers. I didn't stay with a dude long enough for him to get caught up. When they got caught up, that's when we started having problems. Dealing with Tony and his issues was enough for me. I didn't need a man on the street giving me problems too.

I turned off my laptop and placed it on the side of the king-sized bed and eased under the satin covers. My hand located what I wanted. Casper's dick was long and hard and ready for me, but I wasn't quite ready for him.

SWIPE

We kissed. Not the kind of kiss that says I love you, but the kind of kiss you do when you want to fuck. While kissing, Casper used one hand to play with my pussy. He soon replaced his hand with his mouth and devoured me like a hungry lion. I closed my eyes and pretended he was Tony, and the thought of Tony giving me pleasure caused my entire lower body to shake. I gripped Casper's baldhead with my legs and allowed my juices to fill his mouth.

"Yessss," I screamed, hoping my neighbors next door were gone because I wasn't trying to be quiet.

Casper stopped and looked up at me with his glazed lips and licked them. "You like that?"

I shook my head signaling I did.

He eased up from between my legs and lowered himself. I stopped him with my hand. "Not without a condom."

"Come on, baby. Let me just put the head in. I just want to feel it one good time, and I promise I'll take it out."

Men be killing me with that. Besides, the last thing I needed to do was get pregnant and Tony found out. "Casper, come on now. You spoiling the mood."

Since he was as hard as a brick and didn't want to chance me changing my mind, he reached over to his side of the bed and retrieved a condom from the nightstand drawer. He positioned himself again, and without any opposition from me, he thrust his thick, eight-inch shaft inside of me.

I don't know who was moaning more, him or me, because the sex was good. I mean damn good! He hit every spot. I wrapped my legs around his waist. "Deeper. Go deeper," I insisted.

KAYENNE

He put his back into it and had me creaming all over his dick. He fucked me so good that afterward I fell asleep. When I woke up, Casper was gone. After I showered, I got dressed to go to work at one of the local department stores at the mall. No sooner than I reached the living room did I notice my wallet was half way out of my purse. I pulled the wallet completely out. "No, he didn't steal from me!" I yelled.

I located my cell phone and dialed Casper's number. "I take it you noticed I was gone."

"Yes, you ratchet ass nigga!"

Casper laughed. "I'll pay you back. I promise."

"How you going to pay me back? You don't have a job."

"I do the same thing your man in the pen did, so hang tight. I'm going to flip this, and I'll pay you back with interest."

"That's my car note. I need my money, Casper, and I mean now!"

"Baby girl, too late. I've already made the transaction."

"Casper, you better not come around me again until you have my money." Pissed and upset, I hung up without waiting for him to respond.

Tony could hang it up. He wouldn't be getting fifty more dollars this month, and now I had to figure out what I was going to do about my car note. I didn't want to lose my Honda Accord. I hit the bed with my fist. I couldn't believe I got jacked. Never trust a big dick man with a pretty smile. They'll get you each and every time.

CHAPTER THREE
China Frasier

"Mrs. Sims, did you hear the judge?" Marty Morrison, my overpaid lawyer who apparently failed to do his job, asked.

"Yes, I heard him. Why didn't you object?" Anger filled my body as I looked directly at the Caddo Parish judge.

Marty attempted to whisper, "One thousand a month is good. Plus you get to keep the house. Be glad the judge agreed to give you that."

"That's scrap. Gerry Sims has more money than that. Besides, he's the one who cheated. Not me. Why am I being made to pay the penalty?"

The judge banged his gavel several times. "Morrison, if you don't control your client, she will be detained."

Marty placed his hand on my arm. "Calm down, Mrs. Sims."

"From this day forward, it's Ms. Frasier."

"Ms. Frasier, do you have anything else you would like to say to the court?"

I stood up. "Yes, I got something to say." I looked at Marty, and then at the other table where Gerry sat in his tailor-made three-piece suit looking all smug. "How much did they pay you to rule in his favor?"

KAYENNE

The judge banged the gavel in front of him several times. "Ms. Frasier, you're out of line."

Marty stood up. "Your honor, my client is distraught by this event. Please forgive her for that outburst."

"I meant what I said," I said as Marty pulled on my arm.

Marty said, "I'm trying to keep you out of jail."

My nostrils flared as I sat back down.

"Keep your client under control or else!" the judge threatened.

"She's just venting, your honor."

The judge looked at Gerry and asked, "Mr. Sims, what about you? Do you have anything else you would like to say to the court?"

Marty plastered a huge smile on his face. "No, your honor."

I wanted to walk over to his table and punch him in the face.

"Since the two of you don't have any children together, everything else should go smoothly."

Thank God we didn't have any kids. I didn't want to be tied to him one more minute, let alone life.

The judge continued with the rest of his ruling on my divorce proceedings.

I should have known things would go in Gerry's favor when the judge slipped and called him Gerry as if they were old friends. Come to find out, they actually were. They graduated from the same high school together. And that old saying "birds of a feather flock together" rang true in a situation like this.

SWIPE

The only good thing about today was that I would be free of Gerry. I regret the day I agreed to sign the prenuptial agreement. Now here I am sitting next to this overpriced divorce attorney, left with an expensive house that granted, Gerry still had to pay for, but the utilities cost more than the thousand dollars a month alimony the judge allowed.

"China Frasier, your divorce has been granted. You are officially divorced from Gerry Sims," the judge made his final ruling.

"Yes," I said in victory, in spite of me not winning financially.

When Gerry got caught cheating with our live-in maid, he begged and pleaded with me to not divorce him. I realized then that he didn't love me. He only loved the fact that I was the perfect trophy wife. With my black and white bi-racial features, I could easily fit into his world. My light complexion made me appear to have a year round tan. I worked out consistently to keep my 5-feet 6-inches, medium framed body toned.

Legally, the judge had to grant me something, but he could have given me more. Now, I would be forced to go back to work. I had experience as a bank teller, but if memory serves me correctly, bank tellers still didn't make enough money to keep me on the level I was used to living these past two years.

My attempt to ignore Gerry on the way out was for nothing, because he rushed past everyone and practically beat me to the elevator. "Gerry, you should be happy. You got everything you wanted," I said.

Gerry pressed the button on the elevator. The doors closed. I don't know how we ended up being the only two on the elevator. "China, I didn't get what I wanted. I want you. I want my wife back."

"If you wanted me, you never would have cheated on me."

"I made a mistake. I'm sorry. If you can forgive me, I can stop the judge before he files those papers."

"There's no going back. Besides, the way you screwed me in these divorce proceedings let me know that you don't give a fuck about nobody but yourself."

"That's not true, China, and you know it. I care about you."

"A thousand dollars, Gerry. Really? What the fuck am I supposed to do with that? I spent that much money on clothes every month, but now I'm supposed to pay all the bills on that."

"I'm sorry. If you want to be mad at somebody, be mad at the judge. He's the one who made the ruling."

"At your lawyer's suggestion," I snapped.

By now, we're on the first floor talking and walking.

"China, wait! We can still work this out."

"Gerry, the time to work this out was before you pulled out your dick and stuck it in the maid."

People were staring but I didn't care. Gerry, the prominent businessman, cared about appearances. China, the wife of Gerry, used to care about appearances. But the new China, or should I say the old China—China Frasier didn't give a damn about what anyone had to say. From this day forward, I wouldn't be playing by anyone else's rules. From now on, it's China's rules.

CHAPTER FOUR
Trina

"Biatch, you got my order wrong," some ugly looking woman with a jacked up weave said to me at the drive thru window.

I rolled my neck and said, "You asked for a number three and that's what I gave you."

"A number three is a chicken sandwich, not chicken nuggets," she yelled back.

I handed her a menu. "Now what!" I said under my breath.

"Whatever! I don't want no nuggets. I want my sandwich."

I smiled. "Sure. Pull right up there and someone will bring it out to you." I turned and yelled, "Charles, make me a chicken sandwich with the special sauce and hand it to me when you finish." When we said special sauce, that meant spit on it, throw it on the floor, do whatever disgusting thing you can think of, but put it in the package as if it's fresh because one of us has a customer with a serious attitude.

I'm the wrong person to piss off right now. I've got to figure out how to get my money for my rent, and working up here wasn't going to get it. I'm pissed at myself because I blew off this other guy when I started messing with Ray Ray's ass. From the moment Ray Ray whipped that dick out on me, I became hooked. If it wasn't for the sex I would have been left

KAYENNE

Ray Ray's ass alone. That, and the fact that he had no problems paying my rent, also kept him around.

But one thing I won't tolerate is another woman coming to my house. I got to protect my kids and I can't be having that type of drama around them. People can say what they want about me, but one thing they can't say is that I don't love my kids. Zahara, Yasmin, and Xavier are my heart. Any man I get with got to understand that. I thought Ray Ray did, but obviously he didn't.

I've got to admit his wife is cute in the face, but I can understand why Ray Ray got up with me. Men do tend to love my badonk-a-donk. I'm thin in the waist, but I have a booty big enough to sit a six pack on it.

The way things are going, I might have to use what my mama gave me and go downtown to one of the strip clubs. But then again, my mom would turn over in her grave if her only daughter did that, so now I got to think of something else to make some ends.

"Trina, here's your order," Charles said as he handed me the bag.

"Get the next one," I said, before walking outside to hand the "need a new weave" woman her sandwich. I could hear her bad mouthing me on her cell phone. I didn't care because who was going to get the last laugh in at her expense was going to be me.

"Here you go, ma'am," I said as I smiled and handed her the bag.

"It's about time." She snatched the bag from my hand and peeled away, barely missing the car that was turning into the parking lot.

The rest of my day went by uneventful. Tired of being on my feet, I couldn't wait to relax. I clocked out and jumped in my blue older model Camry. It was only spring but this Louisiana heat was kicking in already. My air conditioner worked in spells. Today was one of those days it didn't want to work. I rolled down my window to feel some air. I turned the radio on to KMJJ and bopped my head to a Lil Boosie song as I drove down West 70th Street toward my house.

I almost didn't hear the phone ring over the loud music. "What's up, Mia?" I asked while driving and attempting to turn the music down.

"Can you swing by my place?" she asked, sounding upset.

"I can't stay long. I need to be home when the kids get off the bus."

"It won't take long. I just don't feel like having this conversation on the phone."

I made a U-turn at the next light which was Linwood and went two blocks to Mia's apartment. I found a parking spot right near her apartment.

Tired feet and all, I slowly made my way up the flight of stairs to the second floor. She didn't live in the projects, but she didn't live in a luxury apartment either. The apartment complex was two blocks away from a middle school. A diverse set of people were living in the complex: Those that worked and those that were on government assistance.

There was a time when Mia lived in a three-bedroom house, but since her man went to jail, she downgraded. Tony was one of the biggest dope dealers in the city, so I don't know what happened to all of his money. But Mia's my girl, so here I am.

Mia must have been on the lookout for me because the front door to her apartment swung open before I could knock. She pulled me inside. "Trina, I know you got your own things to pay, but I need a favor."

"No hey girl, what's up? How you doing? Ray Ray still getting on your nerves? None of that?" I asked. The last time Mia asked me for a favor, I almost got my ass kicked.

The inside of her apartment looked better than the outside. She downsized from her house but she kept a lot of her expensive furniture. I plopped down on her plush brown couch and waited for her to respond.

"Girl, I'm sorry. I'm stressing over here. The store cut my hours. I got a car note to pay and this ninja Casper jacked my money I was going to use. I'm already two months behind."

"So you want me to go help you find him?"

"Nah, that ain't going to do any good." Mia told me what happened with Casper and her money.

"That's fucked up."

"I can't tell any of Tony's friends about it because then they'll know I was fucking around on their boy. And then you know what kind of shit that will cause."

"They'll be trying to beat your ass."

"I know, that's why I got to let it ride. Do you think you can get some money from Ray Ray? I promise to pay you back."

"Chile, please. Me and Ray Ray ain't even talking." I told her what happened.

Mia looked disappointed. "I don't know what I'm going to do."

I shifted in my seat. I don't know why I didn't think about this before, but I knew exactly how Mia could solve her financial problem, and it could

SWIPE

possibly help me with mine too. Mia wasn't going to like it, but she didn't have a choice and neither did I.

KAYENNE

CHAPTER FIVE
Mia

Going to Trina was my last choice, but everyone else I went to who owed me favors all claimed they didn't have anything to give or loan me. In the past, I was the one always giving folks money, but that's when Tony was on the streets and he kept my pockets overflowing with cash.

With me about to be two months behind on my car note, the used car dealership would be threatening to repo my car and I didn't want to be left depending on the SPORTRAN bus to get me around. I wiped the sweat from my face with my hand.

"Mia, did you hear me?" Trina asked.

I'd zoned out so I hadn't. "What you say?"

"I know how we can solve your problem."

"I'm down for anything." I could kick Tony's ass for leaving me like this. All of the money he made from selling drugs was confiscated. I wouldn't be in this situation if he had listened to me and put at least half of it in an account that I still had listed under my maiden name that the law knew nothing about. Everything in our joint account was taken. Just like that. So if it wasn't for my infrequent deposits in my second account, I would have been ass out on the streets a long time ago.

SWIPE

Tony still had money hidden somewhere, but he wouldn't tell me the location. He'd been blowing up my phone ever since he didn't get that fifty dollar money order, but I didn't care. I hadn't answered the phone. I still blame him for having to leave my beautiful three-bedroom home and come back to this. I live okay, but nothing like I used to live. He promised to take me out of the hood and here I am, right back here. So fuck him.

"I just filled up my tank, so I guess I'll drive out to Cross Lake," Trina said.

"Why we got to go way over there?" I asked.

"You must be smoking that crack. You act like Cross Lake is in a whole different parish. It's still in Shreveport. Besides, China lives there. She might be able to help us both out."

"Oh, hell no! That bitch will never see me beg her for shit."

"Trina, you got to let that shit go."

"We were girls. Then she up and married that white man and forgot all about us. She acted like we didn't exist."

"I know you didn't." Trina rolled her neck. "When you got with Tony, you up and moved out the hood, so don't even go there."

"But I still came back to hang out. Where was she?"

"She came back too. You just wasn't here to see that."

"She had my number. She should have reached out."

"Bitch, please. You used to change your number like bitches change drawers."

26

KAYENNE

Trina had a point. Tony was so paranoid about being caught that he constantly had our phone numbers changed. It didn't do any good because one of his boys from the inside snitched on him, and he ended up catching a case behind his testimony.

"Whatever. China could have reached out to me if she wanted to, so fuck China."

Trina stood up. "Fine. You can sit your broke ass down there if you want to, but after I go pick up my kids, I'm taking a ride to Cross Lake. It's time X, Yas, and Za saw their other godmother."

Trina left me on the couch in my own misery. China used to be my girl. We used to get in and out of trouble growing up. People always assumed that she got her light, almost near white-skinned complexion from her mother, but it was totally opposite. Her mother was black and her dad white. He died in some war, so her mom moved back from California into our Cedar Grove neighborhood, which is the same neighborhood her mother grew up in as a child herself.

I was the one who used to take up for China when the kids would tease her. We soon became best friends. We did everything together. Our mothers were both single parents and took turns making sure we went to school and other functions. We met Trina in junior high. She stayed a few streets over and ever since then we'd been tight.

Our mothers did their best raising us, but it still didn't stop us from liking the bad boys. If he wasn't a doughboy we didn't want him. We liked being the popular girls in school. We liked wearing the dopest clothes and having money to buy whatever we wanted. Back then, we all thought we were living the good life.

All of that changed when China got a scholarship to college and went to LSU in Baton Rouge. When she came back home after her second semester, she seemed to be a different person. We still hung out, but her love for the streets had dwindled because she stopped dating street dudes and went for the more sophisticated type.

Trina and I were both shocked when she came back home after graduating from LSU with a huge rock on her finger. Not only had she gotten engaged, but married, yet neither Trina nor I was in the wedding.

Our friendship hadn't been the same since. Trina could forgive her, but as for me, well I didn't want anything bad to happen to her, but that bitch broke the friend code and for that, I didn't know if I could forgive her.

A Hurricane Chris ringtone rang on my phone, bringing me back from my trip down memory lane. "UNKNOWN" displayed on the caller ID. I checked the message afterward. The man at the used car dealership was calling about my payment. A payment I didn't have. Then I thought about what Trina said. I thought about China. I picked up my cell phone and dialed Trina's number. "Swing by here and pick me up. I'm going with you to China's. Besides, that bitch owes me. She owes me big time."

KAYENNE

CHAPTER SIX
China

My first week back at Weinstein Bank and Trust was boring. I wasn't a teller because all of the positions were filled. Mr. Belk, my old supervisor, was now branch manager, so he created a position for me. I was to enter customers' information for those who came in wanting a loan. He called the position, loan assistant. I just called it data entry. Fortunately, I have a college degree, or I wouldn't even have that position. I guess it's better than nothing until I could figure out what else I was going to do.

I fired my jack-legged lawyer. Maybe I should get another one and dispute the settlement and see if I can get more alimony. I'm still pissed about that. I felt my blood pressure rising, so I eased further down into the bubble bath inside my huge sauna, an oval-shaped porcelain tub. The water relaxed me. I thought I heard the doorbell, but I wasn't expecting anyone, so I closed my eyes. There the noise was again. This time there was no mistaking the ringing doorbell. I eased up out of the tub and dried off.

After I removed the long, pink terry cloth plush robe from the door hanger, I wrapped it around my body. I eased into my matching slippers and went down the cascading stairs. I couldn't make out the person's impression through the stain-glassed windows on each side of the front door.

The doorbell rang once more. Whoever was on the other end was very persistent, so much so they were getting on my nerves. I didn't even bother to look through the peephole. I yanked the door open.

"Yeah, what do you want?" I asked, coming face to face with five faces I hadn't seen in a very long time.

Trina spoke out. "Bitch, you know who it is."

We used to use the word "bitch" as a term of endearment, although some frowned upon its use. I don't normally use the word now, unless I really think a man or a woman is being a "bitch."

Trina and I hugged.

"Hey, girl, " I said, genuinely happy to see her.

The faces of my god children stared back up at me. I felt a little guilty because since being with my husband, I mean ex-husband, I'd fell in some of my duties. I still did the birthday and Christmas gifts, but I could have done better.

"My three favorite kids."

"Hi Auntie China," they each said as they hugged me.

"Come on in," I said.

I could feel Mia staring at me behind those huge black designer shades of hers, but she didn't say anything. I turned and looked at her. She was wearing a multi-colored form-fitting short dress. "How you going to come in my house and not say anything? What's up?"

Mia responded half-heartedly, "Hey."

KAYENNE

Trina grabbed me by the arm. "Don't pay her any attention. She's going through some things."

"Aren't we all," I responded.

"I hope we're not disturbing you and thangs. We know you got your own thang going on, so we don't wanna be here too long."

"Auntie China, do you still have that dog?" Xavier, with his big pretty doe eyes, asked. He's going to be a lady killer when he grows up.

"No, baby. Unfortunately, Bubbles is in doggy heaven. One day I plan on getting another dog, and I'll let you play with him or her."

"Mama, can we get a dog?" he asked.

"No. See what you started, China."

From the corner of my eye I watched Mia walk around as if she were inspecting things. I noticed her picking up pictures on my mantle and then placing them down. The snarl on her face remained. I didn't know what her problem was, but I was about to become a problem solver and find out. She came to my house. I didn't come seeking her.

"Y'all want something to eat?" I asked. "I just got here, but I can whip us up something real quick."

"We don't plan on being here that long," Mia responded.

"She talks, people," I said.

Mia stopped being nosy and looked up at me.

Trina asked, "Is there some place the children can go? I . . . I mean, we really need to talk to you about something."

I looked at Mia and then back at Trina. "Sure. You two have a seat and I'll be right back. Come on, kids. Let me take you to the game room."

SWIPE

I could hear Mia mumble something, but I just couldn't make out what she said as I directed the kids to the game room. "Y'all stay in here until someone comes to get you."

"Yes, ma'am," Yasmin responded.

Before I walked out, I said, "Come on. Y'all give your auntie another hug."

They hugged me. I closed my eyes. I felt the love. I missed them. *I can't believe I let so much time pass.* I couldn't believe I allowed Gerry to control my life that I stopped fooling with my friends, but I guess I couldn't blame him for everything. I could have visited them more often. Growing up in the hood left me with some fond memories, but it also had some memories that I wished would go away. Some things happened that not even my girls knew about.

I snapped out of it as I heard the sound of the kids getting excited with the numerous choices they had. Right then I promised myself that I would take a more active role in their lives. "Have fun."

Before going back into the living room with Mia and Trina, I went upstairs and slipped on a pair of jogging pants and an LSU T-shirt.

I stopped in the doorway of the living room and watched Trina and Mia for a moment. It's as if they sensed I was there. They looked at me. I walked around and sat in the chair across from them and looked in their direction. I had to let them know that although I lived a better life now, that I was still China from the Grove. "I know this isn't a social visit, so what do you bitches want?"

KAYENNE

CHAPTER SEVEN
Trina

China hadn't lost her edge. She was surrounded by all these fancy things, but she still had a little hood in her. That's what I'd been trying to tell Mia, but she wasn't having it. Mia would never admit it, but I think she's jealous of China for going to college and getting out of the hood the legal way.

Who am I to judge? I've lived in the hood all of my life. I'm happy in the hood. As long as I have a roof over my children and my head and food on our table, I'm straight. Mia and China were the ones who always wanted to live like princesses. Don't get me wrong, I like to look fly too, but my desires had nothing to do with materialistic things.

"Where's your husband?" Mia asked.

I kicked her on her leg.

"Ouch!" Mia said as she bent down to rub her ankle.

"China, you don't have to answer that if you don't want to," I responded.

China stood up. "Does anyone else need a drink?"

"I'll take something." I held my hand up.

Mia moved my hand. "You're driving. I'll take hers. She'll have water."

"Two glasses of Cognac and a bottled water coming."

"How y'all going to dictate what I drink?"

They both ignored me. China walked back in holding a tray. She handed me a cold bottle of water and Mia her drink. She took the remaining drink and sat down.

I watched her take a big gulp before pouring herself some more. "Ladies, it's been awhile, so let me give you the condensed version. Gerry and I are no longer together."

"Really?" Mia acted like she really cared.

"I caught his ass in the bed with our maid so he had to go."

"Niggas will be niggas," I responded.

"The bitch ass judge went to school with him and tried to screw me. I got the house"—She raised her hand up—"and a little alimony."

Mia leaned back on the sofa and crossed her legs. "At least you're going to be riding pretty. This is a big damn house. I could stay here and never leave." She glanced around the room.

"It takes some money to upkeep this baby too," China responded. She placed her glass on the tray that now sat on the table.

"Sorry to hear things didn't work out with you and Gerry. You always seemed so happy," I stated.

"I thought we were too, up until I saw the maid sucking his dick."

"You know you have to slob on the knob," Mia said.

China addressed Mia. "I was like his very own porn star. He had no reason to look elsewhere."

KAYENNE

"Excuse me," Mia responded.

"I'm just saying. I'm twenty-three, fine and flexible, but he cheats with this old woman who's in her thirties. I'm like dude, really. Pissed me the fuck off."

"China, you ain't the only one with men problems. I found out my so-called man has a wife. I'm like: how do you forget to tell someone you're married? Come on now. Where they do that at?"

Mia sipped on her drink and said, "At least your husband didn't leave you destitute like mine did. Bitch got money but won't tell me where he's hidden it. Talking about the Feds might be watching me. Fuck him and the Feds."

"Mia, I read about what happened to Tony in the paper," China said.

"Then, why didn't you call me? That would have been the perfect time to reach out to a sista."

"Because I was too caught up in my own drama. Trying to be a wife to a man like Gerry was a full time job. Y'all just don't know."

"I would trade positions with you any day," I said, looking around the room and admiring how it was decorated. Looked like it could be one of those celebrity houses with the high ceilings and expensive looking furniture. I could see my kids and me living a life of luxury.

"All that glitters ain't gold. Believe that." China shifted in her seat. "But enough talk about men. I know y'all didn't make no special trip to tell me your relationship woes. What's really on your minds?"

Mia blurted, "Since it was Trina's idea, I'll let her tell you."

SWIPE

I rolled my eyes at Mia. Leave it to Mia to push me under the bus. We're best friends, but sometimes she makes me wonder.

"Well, we didn't know you were going through a divorce and thangs, so maybe this isn't a good idea."

"Oh no, you didn't drag me all the way over here and we leave without saying something," Mia blurted out.

China looked at Mia and then at me. "Just say it. I've had a long day and I'm tired."

"Well . . ." I started saying.

Mia took over the conversation. "We needed to know if you could loan us some money. My car is about to get repo'd and if Trina don't get money by the first, her landlord will be kicking her and those three beautiful kids of hers out on the streets."

Mia looked at me. "Now was that hard?"

"No," I responded. "But you didn't have to be so blunt."

China eased to the edge of her seat. "That's okay. You know Mia's always been like that."

"So are you going to give it to us, or did we make a wasted trip?" Mia asked.

China stood up and walked out of the room without saying a word.

"Mia, why you have to be so rude? You should have let me ask her. Now we're both going to walk out of here empty handed."

"I'm not kissing up to her or nobody else. I didn't even want to come."

"But you did, so shut the fuck up. When China gets back, stop with the fucking attitude."

KAYENNE

"Trina, you forgot who you talking to. You get around China and now you want to show out."

"I'm just saying. Chill. We both need this."

Mia rolled her eyes and leaned back and crossed her arms.

China returned holding two envelopes and her iPad. "You can have this on one condition."

Mia uncrossed her arms. "What?"

"Agree to listen to a plan I just came up with."

"I can do that. You, Trina?" Mia asked.

"Of course. No problem," I responded.

China smiled and handed us each an envelope.

CHAPTER EIGHT
Mia

I checked the envelope and saw several one hundred dollar bills. Ten to be exact. That was enough to get my car note caught up plus leave a few hundred in my pocket. I folded the envelope and placed it inside my bra. I patted it to make sure it was secure.

Trina and China were both staring at me. "Thank you, China," I said through gritted teeth.

"You're welcome," China responded, as she sat down across from us in the chair.

This time she was doing something on her iPad. I hope she didn't want us to sign some contract saying when we were going to pay her back. I might need to hand her back the extra money because at this point I'm not sure when I'll be able to repay her.

"What I didn't tell you is that my asshole of an ex-husband only has to pay me one thousand dollars a month," China said.

"That's fucked up," I said.

Trina said, "You must have had one of those court-appointed attorneys. He screwed you."

"I might as well have, because in the end, I felt like he was working for my husband instead of me. The judge did require my husband to pay my legal fees."

KAYENNE

China told us what occurred during her court proceedings. A part of me felt bad that she got screwed, but another part of me was like: karma is a bitch. So now she's back working just like Trina and me, but at least she has a better job.

I wish I didn't have to be on my feet servicing ungrateful people, and I'm not even talking about the customers. I'm talking about my co-workers, who try to act like they better than me because they're in a supervisor position.

China looked back and forth between Trina and me. "I think I have a way we all can make a little money. Well, a lot of money if we play it right."

I still hadn't forgiven China for abandoning her friends, mainly me, but making money, now she had my attention. "I'm listening," I said.

China continued talking. "Remember how we used to boost from the stores?"

Trina responded first. "Yes, but every time I felt like I was gonna have a heart attack because I just knew we were going to get caught."

"We almost did one time until China flirted with the security guard and he let us go."

"I vowed never to do that shit again. At that time I had just had the triplets. I was afraid I wasn't going to be around to take care of my kids," Trina said.

"Well, the plan I have is sort of like boosting but on another level, and if we do it right, it will erase all of our money woes."

"Count me in," I blurted. I didn't have to hear the details. I needed to get back to living ghetto fabulous because dodging creditors on the phone was for the birds.

"Trina, what about you?" China asked.

"I got to think about my kids," she responded.

China's eyes seemed to light up. "That's just it. If you agree to do this with us, you'll be providing for your kids."

Trina shrugged. "I'll think about it."

China continued to talk. "This is what came to me while I was getting dressed upstairs. In my new position, I have access to a lot of information. In fact, each one of us is in position to get information."

"How is that?" I asked.

China broke it down. "Mia, you work at a department store, right?"

"Yeah, so what?"

"Most people use credit or debit cards to pay for their items."

"I still don't get it," I responded.

"Let me finish and it'll come together." China looked away from me and then looked at Trina. "You're still working at the drive-thru?"

"Unfortunately, yes," Trina responded.

"As I started off saying, we're all in some good positions to get information." China turned her iPad around so that we could see what she was looking at too. "This scanner records information. I'm going to order one for each of you."

Trina said, "I don't know what to do with that thang."

China said, "As soon as they come in, I'll need for y'all to come back out here and then we can practice using it. Mia, text my number so I'll have yours."

I pulled out my cell phone and sent a text to the number China rattled off. "You still haven't told us how using those machines is going to make us money."

"That's just part of it," China said. "We will need a few more people to work with us. But it must be people we can trust. I've been out of touch lately, so this is where I'm going to depend on the both of you to help out."

"After what happened to Tony, I don't trust anyone but myself."

Trina sighed out loud. "Oh, really?"

"You know what I'm saying. Friends will turn on ya. Right, China?"

"Mia, I'm sorry. Are those the words you need to hear to get over it?" China blurted out.

"You can keep your lame apology." Forget China and her plan. I headed to the car.

CHAPTER NINE
China

Mia always had an attitude problem and today was no different. She just got up and walked out in the middle of our conversation. We were all grown women, so I didn't have time to babysit her or monitor all of her mood swings.

Trina said, "China, I know you think Mia's tripping, but she was hurt when you stopped coming around."

"I kept in touch," I responded.

"Yes, but not much."

I couldn't deny what Trina said. I did stop hanging out much. Going away to college made me realize there was more to life than scheming and trying to pull the baddest dude in the neighborhood. I wanted to use my brains instead of my body to get ahead. I laughed out loud. My business degree was about to get put into full use because I was determined to do whatever I needed to do to make sure my plan worked.

First step was to go outside and talk to Mia.

"I'll be right back. Go check on the kids," I told Trina.

I went outside. Mia was leaning on the hood of Trina's car. Her shades were now on top of her hair.

KAYENNE

She was looking down at her phone. It appeared as if she was texting someone.

"I'll be off your property as soon as my friend comes to pick me up," Mia blurted without looking up at me.

"Text them and tell them you've changed your mind," I said.

She looked up with her lips pouted. "I need to get as far away from you as I can."

"Why? Because you're mad because I made it out and you're still there."

"If I wasn't afraid of catching a case, I would jump your ass right now," Mia stated.

"You might beat me, but I sure ain't going down without a fight. You might walk away, but not without some scratches and some bite marks."

Trina chuckled. I didn't know she was behind me. Trina said, "You two are a trip. Kiss and make up so we can make that money."

I looked at Mia. "She's right, you know. Let's leave the past in the past."

Mia typed something on her cell phone. She stood up straight and walked right past Trina and me and back into my house.

She was seated on the sofa by the time we went inside.

"Now, where was I before Miss Thang decided to walk out?" I said.

Mia said, "Let's get this straight. Just because I'm agreeing to this plan of yours. It does not mean we are buddy buddy."

"Whateva. As far as I'm concerned we still girls, but I'm not about to kiss your ass. I apologized, so there's nothing else for me to say."

Trina talked with her hands as she spoke. "Forget the drama and let's be about making our bread."

"Yes, let's table it."

Mia shifted in her seat, but remained quiet.

"We will need someone to make us some fake IDs, among other things. Mia, do you still know how to get in contact with Chip?"

"I see him every now and then. I can reach him, but Tony's not going to like that," Mia responded.

"Do you tell your husband everything?" I asked.

She shook her head from side to side.

"That's what I thought. Get me Chip's contact info."

"I can give it to you now," Trina said.

"I didn't know you and Chip stayed in contact," Mia said, looking at Trina.

"He gave it to me to give to you. I never erased it from my phone." Trina got her phone and scrolled through her contacts.

I held my phone up and bumped hers. It automatically transferred the contact information to my phone. "Thanks. I'll call and see if I can set up a meeting with him. As soon as the machines come in, we'll be all set."

Trina threw her hands up. "You still haven't told us what we supposed to do."

"When the machines come in, I'll tell y'all everything y'all need to know. For now, make plans to meet back over here in three days. By then, the machines should be here and it'll give me enough time to talk to Chip."

Reluctantly, they both agreed. As soon as they left my house, I dialed Chip's number. We set up a time to meet. We would meet at Betty Virginia Park, located in an area far from either one of our neighborhoods. I placed the order for the machines and went to bed.

The next day after work, I met Chip at the park. He still looked the same, except bigger. I can see why Mia fell for him back in high school. His round baldhead was perfectly shaped. A goatee adorned his brown face. He was rubbing it as I approached. He stood up from the bench and gave me a tight hug. "Look at you. Haven't seen you in the hood in a long time," Chip said, after releasing me.

We both took a seat next to each other on the park bench.

"Been busy with school and you know I tried the marriage thing."

"Where the rock at?" He held up my hand and noticed my finger was minus a wedding band.

"I had to let that go. That didn't quite work out for me."

"His loss. Someone else's gain."

"Maybe, but I got other things on my mind right now," I said.

"So what's up?"

I patted Chip on the hand. Anyone passing by would think we were a couple. I looked around to make sure nobody was nearby so they wouldn't overhear our conversation.

"You still good with computers?"

SWIPE

"Is fat meat greasy?"

"I have a proposition for you."

"Whatcha got, baby girl?" Chip asked.

"I'm going to need some fake IDs. Not just any IDs, but they need to look state issued. When I put in a request, I will need quick turnarounds. Do you think you can handle that?" I asked.

"I can handle it, but can you handle my price is the question," Chip responded.

"I'm sure we can work it out." I flashed my kilowatt smile.

"So what do you need the IDs for?" Chip asked.

I went with my gut instinct and decided to trust Chip. If my plan was going to work, I needed him to do me another favor. I shared with him a little more information.

"I got you covered. I can take care of all that. We just need to get a system in place that can't be traced."

"Let me think on that and I'll get back with you," I responded.

Chip licked his lips. "No worries. I gotcha. You just need to do your part."

"Then it's a deal."

He placed his big strong hands around mine and shook it. My body felt an electric current flow through it, and from the shocked expression on his face, I could tell he felt it too.

Chip's cell phone beeped, breaking our trance. He glanced at it. "Baby girl, I got to go." He reached into his pocket and handed me a card. "For our business, use this number. I suggest you use it from another phone besides your own."

KAYENNE

He was right. For what we were about to do, we all needed new phones. Phones that would not be able to be traced back to us. I made a mental note to make a special trip to the store for that. *Operation Make That Money* was in full effect.

CHAPTER TEN
Trina

I couldn't help myself, so I kept looking over my shoulder checking to make sure no one saw me put the scanner on the other side of the register. China received them two days ago and instructed Mia and me on how to use them. Fortunately for me, the only cameras we had were on the outside of the building and none were on the inside.

My manager finally left for the day, so I could put it there without her noticing. I just had to remember to remove it before the next shift manager got there.

I took the orders through the drive thru like I normally did. The man driving a Mercedes seemed so engrossed in his phone conversation, he barely looked at me as I gave him his total. He practically threw me his credit card. I ran the Visa through the cash register, and then I ran it through the machine I had attached. The receipt printed from the register, and I attached it to his bag of food. I handed him the receipt and the bag.

A woman with several little kids screaming in the back drove up to the window. I repeated the same thing.

"Trina, the schedule's been posted," I heard Charles say from behind me.

KAYENNE

I jumped. "Fuck, Charles. Next time don't be sneaking up behind me like that."

"You tripping. You need to get those headphones out your ear and then you can hear." Charles went back to the cooking area.

I looked around to see if anyone else was nearby. One of my co-workers handed me a bag. "It's with no onions like requested."

"Thanks," I responded with a smile.

This person paid with cash, so I didn't get the opportunity to use the machine.

I checked the clock. Only fifteen more minutes before the evening shift supervisor came on. I tapped my foot, anticipating the next car.

"Can you give me some extra ketchup because the last time y'all didn't put nothing in there," the gray-haired woman said.

She was old enough to be my grandmother, so I decided not to swipe her card in the machine when she gave it to me. I handed her the bag with the extra ketchup.

After I slipped the machine under my jacket, I went to the back and located my bag where I kept my personal items. I placed the machine in it.

"Trina, it ain't break time. Get your behind back on that register," Shan, the evening supervisor, said near the door.

I coughed. "I was looking for a cough drop."

"Find it and get back to the drive thru."

"Bitch," I mumbled as I zipped up my bag and placed it back where it was.

I rolled my eyes as I passed her. I hoped what I was doing was going to put a lot of food on my kids' and my table, because people like Shan were the reason I hated coming to this place.

Shan ain't shit as far as I'm concerned. The only reason she got the promotion is because she'd been fucking the manager. If it hadn't been for that, I would have gotten the position. He tried to get me to sleep with him, but wasn't no way I could bring myself to sleep with his short, ugly, limped-dick ass.

I was desperate, but not that doggone desperate. Just the thought of him made me want to throw up.

The girl working the drive thru moved and I got back to work. An hour later, I was on my way home. The kids' school bus had already come down our street. My three munchkins were waiting for me on the porch.

"Za, looks like I need to give you a key just in case I'm running late again," I said after hugging them.

"Why Za gets the key? Why not me?" Yasmin asked.

Zahara put her hand on her hip, imitating me. "Because I'm the oldest."

I tried not to laugh as I slipped the key in the lock and we all walked in. I flipped the light switch on, but nothing happened. "Shit . . . damn . . ." were words that slipped out of my mouth. I'd forgotten to pay the other part of the light bill.

"Mama, what happened to the lights?" the always so observant Xavier asked.

"X, you ask too many damn questions. Y'all go put your back packs up and let's go. Mama got to go run an errand."

KAYENNE

I went to my bedroom and pulled up a loose floorboard under my bed. Because I didn't have a bank account, that's where I kept my money when I had any. I retrieved a hundred dollar bill out of the envelope China had given me the week before. I made sure the rest was secure.

The kids were waiting for me at the car when I stepped outside. Two hours later, they were in the room playing and keeping up noise as usual. China was seated next to me on the couch.

China said, "I haven't heard from Mia yet, so I don't know how her day went."

"I only got three cards."

"That's good. Tomorrow try to get more."

"Chip is going to make us some IDs."

China typed in a code on a website on her laptop. "Okay, try to get just women's cards because this one is a dude." She showed me what she was looking at.

My mouth flew open. "Wow. That's all of their information. How did you get that?"

China looked around to make sure the kids hadn't slipped in the room. "I told you the device would scan all the necessary information. I'm going to pass this info to Chip, and then we'll be in business. I need you to put this on so I can take your picture."

China pulled out a short black wig. It was hard fitting my braids under it but I did. "How do I look?"

"It's too bulky. Try this one." China removed another wig. It was a little longer and thicker.

"I can make this work." China held up my braids as I put the wig on. "What about this?"

"Better. But girl, I ain't trying to tell you how to do your hair, but you gonna have to get those braids

51

out. We need to have different looks. Check your mailbox when you get up in the morning. You'll have an ID in it. You need to go get a post office box set up with the name on it. Give them this address for a physical address on the application if they require you to have one."

China snapped my picture with her phone. She then left. I fixed dinner for the kids, ignored Ray Ray's calls and went to bed. The next morning, I checked the mailbox as China instructed and an envelope was in there. The ID had the same name as one of the customers. I went directly to the post office as soon as the kids were on the bus. I made sure I wore the same wig that was on the picture.

"Ms. Dell, I will need to see your ID, please," the post office clerk said.

I eased the ID out of my purse. With sweaty palms, I handed it to him.

"Ms. Dell, looks like we have a problem."

He looked at the ID and then back at me. I knew it. I knew this wasn't going to work. I held my breath.

CHAPTER ELEVEN
Mia

China's plan seemed to be working. Wearing different wigs, we all got fake IDs made under different names and got post office boxes at post offices across the city. I'd dragged myself out of bed to get to work this morning. I'd put on what I call my Beyoncé wig and one of my designer dresses I bought during the time Tony was out on the streets. I normally would have worn some stilettos with the dress, but knowing I would be on my feet for at least six hours made me change my foot gear to something more comfortable like some black flats.

Usually I worked in the clothing department by myself. Before heading to my post, I flirted with one of the guys in security. He proudly allowed me into his work space. "The cameras rotate from department to department. See, that's your department there." Sam, the potbellied security guard, pointed to the monitor. My eyes scanned the screen, and my mind calculated how much could be seen on screen.

"So you sit and watch me all day?" I asked as I made sure my booty rubbed up against his leg.

"I wish I could, but with reports and having to also watch the dressing rooms, I can't."

"Aw. I thought I had me a secret admirer."

SWIPE

"I admire you and it's no secret," he responded as he licked his lips.

"Well, I like having admirers." I pulled on my tight dress.

"Umph. You got a man?" he asked. "I get off about an hour after you do. Maybe we can go grab something to eat or something."

I conveniently flashed my hand showing my bling. "I wish I could, but I don't think my husband would like that too much."

"Oh, my bad. I didn't know you were married. I've never seen you with a dude. I know if you were my woman, I would be coming up here checking up on you all the time."

I coughed and cleared my throat. "Let's just say my husband is on vacation right now. He has the type of job that keeps him away from home a lot."

"If you ever get lonely . . ." He paused and then stopped when we heard the door open.

"Sam, you know we're not supposed to have anyone else back here," his co-worker said.

I stood straight up. "It's not his fault. I thought I caught someone stealing, but I was mistaken. The customer had a receipt, so we were just talking about the incident," I lied.

"Oh. Oh. I thought this was something else," the gray haired man stuttered.

"What? I'm a married woman. Why would I be in here for that?" I pretended to be offended.

Sam responded, "No need to write up a report for that."

"Good. Thanks Sam for your help, again." I looked at Sam and then stared down the elderly security guard as I left out of the control room with a huge smile on my face.

Upon arriving at my post, I waited until the coast was clear to pull out my clear bag that contained my make-up bag that held the small device. I eased it out and placed it near the register outside of camera view.

I wouldn't have to worry about another sales associate using the cash register once I signed on to it, so I was ready and set to go.

"Ma'am, can I pay for all of this over here? I don't feel like waiting in that long line over in the kid's department," a middle-aged woman wearing a jogging suit said, as she plopped all of her items on the counter.

"Will this be cash or credit?" I asked, before giving her a response.

"Credit. My husband's going to complain about the bill, but then again, if he never sees the bill he can't complain, now can he?" She laughed at her own joke.

Little did she know the joke was on her, because after scanning her Visa card to pay for the clothes, I scanned it on the little device that recorded all of her information. I watched how she signed her name on the electronic device, and then handed her the card back.

"Thank you for shopping at Kelly's Department Store. We hope to see you back," I said with the friendliest smile I could muster.

"Oh, I will be back. Probably tomorrow because I saw some shoes I like."

"If you do, be sure to stop by and say hi," I responded.

SWIPE

She left and another customer walked up with their items. The majority of my shift went like clockwork. I couldn't wait for this shift to end though, because even with the flats on, my feet were hurting.

A co-worker bombarded her way into my personal space behind the register. "Girl, did you hear about what happened to Theresa?"

"No. I've been busy working. I don't have time for what somebody else is doing," I responded.

"Well, she just got fired."

"For what?" I asked, shifting my body so it would hide the device even more.

"They found out she was giving her friends and family huge discounts."

My heartbeat increased a little. "How did they catch her?"

"She messed up when she gave them discounts on some of the new merchandise. If she would have just stuck to the sales items, the auditor never would have caught it."

"That's her fault. She should have been more careful," I responded.

"Ain't nothing in this store worth me going to jail for," my co-worker stated.

"I feel you on that." I really needed her out of my personal space. I didn't need to hear about someone getting caught doing something illegal when what I was doing was far worse.

"I just wanted you to know because we all started together."

"She knew what she was getting herself into. She should have been more careful," I responded.

KAYENNE

"Dang, girl, you ain't got no sympathy for her, do you?"

"Naw, not really. If you going to do something, plan your shit out."

"I'll work two jobs before I go to jail for stealing."

"I feel you on that."

She looked at her watch. "It's about time for our shift to end anyway. I'm going to ride this last hour out. I'll see you later."

I made sure that Ms. Nosy was way out of eye sight before I eased the device I'd been using to snatch the credit card information and placed it back in my make-up bag and in the clear case under the counter.

When my shift ended, I did my best to avoid everyone. I heard Sam from security call out my name, but pretended like I didn't. I didn't exhale until I was safely behind the wheel of my car. I couldn't shake this uneasy feeling. Was Sam trying to continue flirting, or had the camera caught me with the scanner?

CHAPTER TWELVE
China

Operation Make That Money was going just as I'd planned. Mia and Trina were both getting people's credit card information, and along with the bank customer's information off the loan papers, Chip was able to get duplicate credit cards made for each customer.

I advised Mia and Trina to always change their appearance from their normal look when using one of the fake cards. That way, if by chance someone were to come back and look at video footage, no one would be able to recognize them.

That same day I decided to take a much overdue shopping trip to Dallas. With my subtle jet-black lace front wig on and conservative attire, I headed straight to the Galleria when I hit Dallas city limits. I literally shopped until I dropped, but not as China Frasier. *Jill Harper* bought designer clothes, matching shoes, and a couple of designer handbags. Although I—I mean Jill Harper was already wearing a pair of Gucci shades, Jill purchased a few more designer shades.

"Mrs. Harper, would you like someone to carry the bags to your car?" the sales clerk at Saks asked when I checked out.

KAYENNE

She had to call out the name "Harper" several times before it dawned on me, she was talking to me.

"Oh, no. I got it. I'm a seasoned shopper so I got this."

I stuffed the bags in the trunk of the rental car and went about fifteen to twenty minutes to a boutique that I liked to frequent whenever I was in Dallas. I went inside and saw what I'd come for. The costume jewelry was spectacular. The designs were so fabulous that unless you knew the items weren't made from real jewels, you would think they were.

As soon as I walked in the door, a familiar looking sales clerk greeted me. "Oh, shit," I said to myself. I would be forced to use my real card if she recognized me.

The sales clerk said, "Your face reminds me of a customer that used to come in here all the time. You don't happen to know a Sams or Sims, do you? You two could pass for sisters."

"No," I lied. I had to remember which credit card I was about to use, so I could give her the right name. She saved me the trouble of responding further.

"They say everyone has a twin. Well, how can I help you this evening?" she asked.

"I'm looking for sapphire and ruby replicas."

"Come with me. We just got in a new shipment. I think you'll love it."

I followed her and left out twenty minutes later with another purchase, but this time under Vivica Lee's name.

I'd originally planned on driving back to Shreveport, but after all the shopping I found myself getting tired. I pulled over to the parking lot of one of the many luxury hotels in the Dallas area. Always prepared, I kept an overnight bag with me, so I retrieved it from the trunk of the rental car. I would have used valet parking, but I had too much merchandise in the trunk of my car to trust it to valet.

Everyone greeted me as I made my way into the hotel lobby to check in. This is when my photographic memory came in use. I needed to recall which card would be the best one to use for a situation like this.

"Welcome. How many are in your party?" the hotel reservationist asked.

"Tonight, it'll be just me. I would like a room with a king-sized bed and a mini-bar." I plopped down the credit card as if it was mine.

The reservationist picked up the card. "Mrs. Evans, I will need to see your ID."

"It's Ms. Evans," I responded.

"Oh, I'm sorry Ms. Evans," she apologetically said.

I fumbled through my purse as if looking for my identification. "No problem. I just got a divorce. And I needed a weekend getaway." It wasn't a total lie.

"Where are you from?" she asked.

"Houston."

"You're awfully young to be getting a divorce."

"We married right after high school. I thought we would be together forever, but forever to him was until he could dance under the next girl's skirt." I sniffled a little. I still hadn't pulled out an ID.

"You poor girl. Well, you're still young enough to find you another man and have the family you want."

KAYENNE

I sighed. "This is just not my day. I had my ID, but I must have left it at the store I just came from and they're closed."

I reached for my credit card. "I'll chance driving back to Houston tonight, even though I'm tired."

The reservationist responded, "Oh, no we can't have that. I can still run your card through without it."

"Thank you," I said. "I really appreciate it. All I want to do is get in the bed and try to forget my problems."

She handed me the keys to the room. "Tomorrow will be a better day. Get you some rest now."

I kept the fake depressed look plastered on my face until I opened up the door to my plush hotel suite. She'd given me a room with a hot tub. Less than thirty minutes later, I was easing my tense body into the hot, steamy water that I'd filled with bubbles.

I poured myself a glass of champagne and held the glass up. "Cheers to my award winning acting skills."

My smile turned into a frown. What if one of her managers insisted on proper ID? If they did, I would be in a load of trouble.

My eyes bucked when I heard a knock on the door.

CHAPTER THIRTEEN
Trina

I was sitting on the couch watching an episode of *Love and Hip-Hop*, one of my favorite shows, when Xavier came in giving me straight attitude.

"Mama, when you gonna get me my own room?"

"X, I told you we can't afford to move right now," I responded, half-listening to him.

"If we can't afford it, then how we got all these new clothes and shoes?"

Xavier got my full attention with that comment. At eight years old, he was smart. Sometimes too smart for his own good.

"Mama got a bonus, so if she wanted to spend it on buying you some new clothes, that's my business."

"But . . . but," he stuttered.

"But nothing. Get your little ass out of here and go back in the room and watch TV with your sisters."

I didn't mean to snap at him, but neither he, nor did his sisters, need to be all up in my business like that. Most little kids would have just been happy with the things I'd been buying them lately, like the clothes, shoes and toys. But no, not my son who was like a little man in an eight-year-old body.

He made me miss the fight between Stevie and Joseline. Now I got to wait until next week to watch the rerun. The phone rang. I glanced at the caller ID. That was my girl.

"What's up, Mia?" I said as soon as I answered.

"I'm a few minutes away from your spot. Just checking to make sure you at home."

"Where else I'm going to be with these bad ass kids?"

Mia laughed. "Unlock your door. I'm pulling up now."

I got up and greeted Mia at the door. She was looking like a million bucks. She gave her "Gone with the Wind" fabulous twirl, showcasing her brand new outfit. The cream colored pants suit and leopard print stilettos were on point.

"Girl, where did you get those shoes? I need me a pair," I blurted.

"I'll order you a pair. What size? It's not like I'm paying for it with my own money."

We both laughed and sat down on my new leather burgundy sofa.

Mia ran her hand over the leather near where she sat. "Girl, this is nice."

"Might as well use the money to buy some stuff I wanted. And didn't have to wait for tax time." We high-fived each other.

"If money keeps coming in like this, I'll be able to pay off my car in no time," Mia added.

We chatted for a few more minutes about purchases we'd made.

"I've been trying to get in contact with China, but she's not returning my phone calls," I said.

"Yeah. She's been ghost lately."

"Tomorrow, let's ride out there. I'm off tomorrow," I said.

"I'll take off. I can afford to do so now."

A knock on the door interrupted our conversation. I got up and opened the door without looking outside to see who it was.

"Trina, why haven't you been returning my calls?" Ray Ray asked as he pushed past me and into the house.

"Probably because I didn't want to talk to your ass. Now what the fuck you doing here?" I asked as I folded my arms.

"You ain't got to front in front of your girl."

"Hey to you too, Ray Ray," Mia said. Mia never liked Ray Ray.

"Whatever. I didn't come over here to see you." He turned back toward me. "I came to see my Trina."

Before I could bite my tongue, I snapped, "Yours! I'll never be yours again."

"I left my wife. I realized I couldn't be without you and I left her. So now you got me all to yourself."

I laughed. "Ray Ray, the opportunity to leave your wife was *before* you got with me in the first place."

"But, Trina, you know you miss this dick."

There was some truth in what he said. He used to dick me down, but I don't mess with married men because I don't like dealing with the drama that comes with it. Besides, I want a man of my own.

"Can't you tell she don't want your ass no more, so leave!" Mia snapped.

"Bitch, this between me and my girl, so you need to stay out of it."

Mia jumped up. "I got your bitch. Nigga, I'll fuck you up."

I ran and jumped in between them. "Everybody chill. Mia, I got this. Can you get me something to drink while I talk to Ray Ray?"

Mia remained standing there.

"Please?" I asked.

"Okay. But if that nigga want to jump bad, you know I don't have a problem fighting a bitch or a nigga. Bring it on."

"You better get your girl," Ray Ray said, while Mia walked toward the kitchen.

I laughed to myself, because he wasn't talking any more noise when she jumped up threatening to beat him.

Ray Ray and I were now face to face. "Baby, I miss you. I need you. My wife can't do for me what you do for me."

"In other words she don't suck dick like I do."

"Naw, baby, it's more than that. She's just not you."

I moved away. "Ray Ray, I told you when I met you I didn't want to bring drama into my babies lives. So unless you got a divorce, there's nothing else you and I have to talk about."

Ray Ray's face went into a scowl. He walked around the room and picked up some of the new figurines I'd recently purchased and then placed them back down on the table. Then he looked at the wall decorated with some of the new African art I'd bought from a street vendor. He took a long glance down at the new couch. "I'm just noticing this shit. It ain't been gone a good month and you already got a new nigga. No wonder you don't want no more of Ray Ray."

"I don't know what you talking about. I'm by myself."

"Not with all this new shit you ain't. I'm no fool. You and your new nigga can both fuck yourselves. You ain't got to worry about me running over here to kiss your ass no more."

"Good. Now get to stepping," Mia said, as she re-entered the room holding two wine coolers.

"Fuck you, Mia!" Ray Ray said.

"You wish you could."

"Ray Ray, it's time for you to go. I'm tired of you disrespecting my house like this."

"Fuck you, Trina. You *and* your new nigga. Hope y'all happy. I'm going back home to my wife. At least I know she's loyal to a brother, because you 'hos sure ain't."

"I wasn't a 'ho when I was letting you fuck me every night." I hit him with my hand.

"Trina, I'm warning you. You better keep your hand to yourself."

Mia watched in the background. I hit him again. He grabbed me around the waist.

"Let me go!" I said over and over.

"Not until you stop hitting me," Ray Ray said.

"Okay," I yelled.

Ray Ray placed me down.

"I don't appreciate you calling me a 'ho. I got your 'ho!" I said and went back to hitting him again.

Ray Ray blocked my hits with his hand. "You're crazy." He backed up until he reached the front door.

I stopped hitting him. "Get out!" I said.

KAYENNE

"I'm going, but this ain't over," he said, right before leaving out.

SWIPE

CHAPTER FOURTEEN
Mia

"You have a collect call from 'Tony.' This call may be monitored and recorded. To accept this call press zero," the recorded operator said. I pressed zero before hearing any other options.

"Baby girl, what's going on? I got your letter. Why haven't you been answering my calls?"

"If you got my letter, then you know why. It's been rough on me out here on these streets fending for myself," I responded.

"Your rent paid, right?" he asked.

"I'm straight, but no thanks to you," I snapped.

"Ain't much I can do from in here. You know that."

"You know what you could do to ease my situation." We had to talk in code just in case someone was actually listening in on our call.

"You going to come see me this weekend?" he asked.

"Are you going to tell me what I need to know?" I asked. I kept giving him the opportunity to tell me where he had the rest of his money stashed.

"Do we have to keep going over this? I'm not telling you that. You'll know when I get out."

"So you telling me I got to wait ten more years before . . ." I caught myself before blurting out more.

"You maintaining, so you can wait."

"Fuck you, Tony. No, I'm not coming to see you this weekend. And you want to know why? Because a bitch got to work. I got to work, and I'm not taking off to come see you because you don't give a damn about me!"

"Mia, calm your ass down."

"Calm. Nigga, I'll calm down when I got more money coming in to pay these damn bills. Your ungrateful ass couldn't even thank me for putting one hundred on your books. You want a ride or die chick. Well, shit, I want a ride or die nigga."

The operator interrupted our conversation, "You have one more minute left on this call."

"Mia, baby, stop that. I love you. I wish I could do more, but baby, I just can't."

"Well, call me back when you can."

Without waiting on the phone system to disconnect us, I hung up the phone.

Tony called back several times, but after seeing the prison number displayed on the caller ID, I refused to answer. If he didn't stop, I would hit the five on the phone and block the number where he would never be able to call.

Trina's number popped up on my phone. I answered, "What's up?"

"Oh, you'll answer for her, but you won't take my calls. You need to come see me because obviously, we got some problems we need to work out," Tony snapped.

SWIPE

I tried to hold back saying what I really wanted to say, but Tony was working my last nerve. Typical Tony though. He knew how to get folks to do what he wanted them to do. He no longer had that mind control over me, so I didn't care if he used Trina to call for him. I still had nothing else to say to him.

"Trina, I'm not paying for this call. If you want to waste your money accepting collect calls from Tony, that's your business."

Trina responded, "I'm not in it. Talk to the man. He misses you."

Tony interjected. "Listen to your friend. She understands the pressures I'm under. I love you girl, and I just hate I'm not out there to take care of you like I'm supposed to. For better or worse, remember? Baby, this is the worse. I promise you that."

"Whatever, Tony. I'm just tired. Just tired that's all."

"I know you are, baby girl. But just hang on in there with me. I still got a lawyer trying to overturn the ruling. Don't give up on me now. Please. We've come too far," Tony said.

He's right. I'd invested most of my teen years and early twenties on him. "Fine. But I can't come see you this weekend because I got to work."

"Take off. I'll have one of my boys compensate you for missing working."

"I thought . . ." I caught myself again. I couldn't ask if he still had people working for him on the streets, and he's just now telling me about it. It would have to be a conversation we had in person, but it wouldn't be this weekend because I really wasn't in the mood to see him.

KAYENNE

"Come on, Mia."

"Not this weekend, but I promise you it'll be soon."

The operator interrupted. We ended the call with "I love you."

I yelled, "Trina. Trina."

She didn't respond, so I hung up the phone.

I had an internal tug of war going on. With the extra cash I had stashed away I could easily take off and go see Tony. Me punishing him for not telling me the location of the money also punished myself. I missed holding his hand. I missed the touch of his lips. I missed him holding me in his arms. Tears flowed down my cheeks as I thought about all of the things I missed about my husband. As long as he was confined to prison, my heart had an empty space.

CHAPTER FIFTEEN
China

I still felt the adrenaline from my trip to Dallas. When I heard the knock on my hotel door, I just knew I'd been busted. Fortunately for me, it was just someone bringing me a complimentary bottle of champagne courtesy of the lady at the front desk.

Fast forward a few days later and here I am back in Shreveport and entertaining. I decided to give a small dinner party for some of the mutual friends that Gerry and I had, so they could go back and let him see that I was still living a good life without him.

"There are two ladies in the foyer who said they are friends of yours," the caterer leaned and whispered in my ear.

"Thank you," I responded. "Eat and drink and I'll be right back," I told my guest of ten.

I threw my napkin on the table in front of me, and then followed the caterer out of the dining room.

Mia and Trina stood in the foyer. I would have invited them in for dinner too, but they were not dressed in semi-formal attire like the rest of my guests, and I didn't want them to feel uncomfortable.

"Ladies, you should have called first," I said as I greeted them each with a hug and an air kiss.

Trina responded, "Obviously."

KAYENNE

"I see someone's having a dinner party and we failed to get an invite," Mia so duly noted.

I got between them and looped my arm with each one of theirs and led them to the study and closed the door. "These are some of Gerry's friends. I didn't think you would want to hang out with them."

I moved my arms. "Have a seat. I'll have someone bring you a drink."

"Oh, no you not treating us like *the help*." Mia remained standing.

"Mia, sit your ass down. Ain't nobody treating you like the help. The dinner is winding down anyway. Let me get rid of my guests and then we can talk."

Trina said, "I don't have much time. I got somebody watching the kids."

"It won't be too much longer," I assured them. "In the meantime, make yourselves at home." I left out and closed the door, hoping they would stay in the room. I didn't need my old life mixing with my new life. People were finishing their desserts when I returned to the dining room.

Rose asked, "You were gone an awfully long time. Is everything okay?"

"Yes, everything's fine. Just a minor emergency. I took care of it, but I will need to end the party a little early."

"Oh dear, understood. We're just glad to see that after everything that's happened, you're doing okay," Stacy, one of Gerry's colleagues, responded.

"Stacy, thank you for coming. Just because Gerry and I aren't together does not mean we can't be friends."

"Of course. What happened between you and Gerry is between you two. It doesn't affect our friendship," she assured me.

I walked my guests to the door and hugged each one of them as they left. They could now go back and gossip about me to Gerry. I wasn't naive to think that they wouldn't. In fact, I wanted them to. My mission was completed.

Ten minutes later, I walked into the kitchen and watched as the caterer and her workers went through their cleanup process. "I'll be in my study down the hall when you finish. In fact, give me one of those trays. I'm sure my other guests may be hungry."

"Ms. Frasier, I hope you don't mind, but I already took them a few trays. We had plenty left over, and I thought it would be polite to do so."

"Perfect. Just wrap those up and put them in the refrigerator." I pointed at the huge stainless steel refrigerator. "See me before you leave, and I'll give you the final payment for a job well done."

"Thank you," she responded, and went back to work.

When I returned to the study, Mia and Trina were eating and drinking.

"Girl, this cheese dip here is the business," Trina said as she devoured some cheese and crackers.

"Glad y'all like it. I got one more thing to do, and then y'all will have all of my attention."

"Take your time. 'Cause this food is good," Trina said.

I opened up the desk drawer and removed a blank check from the drawer and wrote out the amount I owed the caterer. I added a hundred dollar bonus for the owner. Normally, I would have tipped more, but when times get rough, tipping is the first thing that has to be curbed.

"So what's up?"

"Since Trina's trying to be all shy, we want to know why you haven't returned any of our calls?"

"I've been busy. Trying to make sure this thing we got going on runs smoothly."

"I got my little system down at work. So far no problems, but uh, I need some more accessible cash. Buying things is fine, but there are some things that only cash can buy," Mia said.

"I agree. That's one of the things I've been working on. Wait right here. Let me go upstairs and get my iPad, so I can discuss a few things with the two of you. It's time that we move our operation up a notch."

Mia responded, "That's what I'm talking about. Let's get that money."

"Each and every day," I responded, before heading upstairs.

CHAPTER SIXTEEN
Trina

Mia was getting on my nerves with her attitude. She still got some type of beef with China and they needed to handle that, but I didn't need to be put in the middle of it. I ate some more food while we waited on China to return.

"I don't know why she thinks she has to run everything," Mia mumbled.

"It was her idea," I said in between bites.

"But still. I got ideas too on how we can make money. Didn't nobody bother to ask me."

"Ain't nobody controlling you. Open up your damn mouth!" I responded. I went to the bar and poured myself a drink. My kids were not with me, so I could get my drink on.

Speaking of kids, one of mine was texting me now. I sent a quick text response back. "Tell your sister to stop fighting or deal with me later," I typed.

"My girls are worse than Xavier. They are always fighting," I said to Mia, just as China walked back in.

China eagerly shared her plans. "Now for this phase, we got to be real careful because this involves other people outside of our circle. We can start placing orders for folks and they pay us cash. The only thing is, I don't want any of us to be the main source or contact. I've asked Chip if he knows someone he can trust that would do it for us."

Mia said, "China, I don't know about that. Chip is already doing enough. Having one of his people take orders and cash. I don't know if I can trust that. I would rather chance it and do it myself, than deal with somebody I don't know."

"What about you, Trina?" China asked.

"I can't be having strangers come in and out of my house with my kids, so I know I don't want to do it. I would rather just get the cash off the credit cards like I've been doing to pay for some of my stuff."

"Mia, you sure you want to be our point person, because if you do . . . If shit go down, you might be the main person they come looking for."

"I'm smart enough to handle mine. I'm already a step ahead of both of y'all. I've been selling stuff to my cousin and her friends."

"What!" China asked, looking just as surprised as I was.

"Yes, had too. I got some things I'm trying to do. Besides, we agreed, or should I say you said, not to take more than a hundred dollars cash advance off the cards."

"I'm glad you said something. But you need to be careful."

"Always that, honey. You ain't got to worry about that."

"Trina, since Mia's going to be doing that, I'm going to need you to amp up getting some of those card numbers. Mia's been getting the bulk of them."

"What y'all don't understand, I can't always use that machine. I have to wait until the right manager is on duty. Some of the managers be all up on you, and then there are a few who couldn't care less what you do, as long as you do your job."

"You're just scared," Mia said.

"Scared ain't got nothing to do with it. Being careless will get your ass locked up. I'm being cautious and I will continue to be. If that ain't enough, then fuck both of y'all." I looked back and forth between China and Mia.

China started talking with her hands. Something she always did when she was agitated. "Fine. Trina, just get the numbers when you can."

"Now that we got that established, I will do my part." I leaned back in my chair.

China got up and pulled out a box from the desk drawer. She handed the box to Mia. "Here's the phone you will use to take all orders. Chip will be dropping off a laptop for you to use to fulfill those orders. No one is to ever see your face or know your name. I need you to stop getting stuff for your cousin and her friends," China said.

"They don't know what I got going on. They think I'm selling stuff out of my closet because I'm broke."

"Fine. Keep it that way. The less people who know about this, the better," China said.

"How are we to get the word out that we're doing this without people knowing we're behind it? How are we going to get customers?" I asked.

"That's where you come in too, Trina," China responded.

"You practically know everybody in the hood. Between you and Chip, I think we won't have any problems getting customers."

I was feeling a little uneasy about it, but thought about the cash rewards if we pulled it off. "Okay. I'm in."

"Let's seal it with a drink."

Mia pulled out a blunt from her purse. "I have a better idea. Let's light it up."

Mia lit the end of the blunt. She took the first puff and passed it to me. I puffed on it and started coughing. "Girl, this that good shit."

"You know it. I copped it from one of Tony's boys."

I looked up at China. "What you waiting on? You know you want some."

"Naw, I'm good."

"Even the President said there's nothing wrong with a little ooo wee," I blurted.

Mia laughed. "Don't beg her. More for us. More for me." She took another puff.

China then snatched the blunt out of Mia's hand. "Bitch, give that to me and let me show you how it's really done." China took a huge puff, held it, and then slowly exhaled. "Now what!"

We spent the next hour smoking some herb and reminiscing about old times. It was good hanging with my girls. It felt like old times, but there was something about China that didn't sit well with me. I stared at her through the smoke.

CHAPTER SEVENTEEN
Mia

I hadn't been able to sleep well since my conversation with Tony, so that's how I ended up at the Madison Parish Detention Center in this damp, cool room filled with other families waiting to see their loved ones who were also locked up. Some were innocent and some not so innocent, like my Tony. Truth be told, if Tony were locked up for all the things he'd been guilty of doing, the judge would have locked him up for life and threw away the key. The drug charge he got was just small potatoes, so I guess he and I should consider ourselves lucky.

Purple was Tony's favorite color. I made sure I was looking cute and wore a short, tight black skirt and a cute purple satin top. My make-up was color coordinated to match. I wore heels because he loved seeing me in heels.

My eyes kept looking at the clock. It seemed like I had been here forever for them to bring him from the back, but I'd only been here for fifteen minutes. We were only allowed a two-hour visit, so they needed to hurry up.

I watched women greet their men as they came through the door, but still nothing. I made sure I found a table near the back, far away from the prying eyes of the guards. Some of the guards would get on my nerves. Tony had shared with me on several occasions on how they tried to make their lives miserable. He did assure me that all of the guards weren't that way, but I could only imagine.

A huge smile swept across my face when Tony appeared at the door. He was trying to get the guard's attention to unlock the door and let him in. I stood up so he could get a good full view of me while he walked my way. He still had the prettiest smile I'd ever seen on a man.

I could feel my pussy walls contracting the closer he got to me. Oh how I yearned to feel him inside me again. He pulled me into a tight embrace the moment he got to me. I heard him inhale, and then he gave me a kiss that almost knocked me off my feet.

We heard the guard at the desk clear his throat real loud.

"Hey baby girl, let me stop because I don't want to get him aroused." He looked down at his crouch. "Or that busta riled up," he said, looking over in the direction of the prison guard.

We sat down. Neither of us let go of the other's hand. He picked up my hand and kissed the back of it. My other hand went up and touched his face. "I've missed you," I said.

"I can't tell by how you talk to me sometimes," Tony responded.

"You just don't know how tough it's been for me since you've been behind these walls."

Tony leaned back and looked at me. "You're looking mighty good from this position, baby girl."

"Whatever."

SWIPE

"You hurt my feelings when you wouldn't come see me the last time I asked you to."

"I couldn't take off work."

He eased his chair closer to mine. "But you're here now, so I won't complain."

"No panties," I whispered.

"Look and see what the guard's doing," Tony responded.

I peeked over Tony's shoulder. The guard wasn't paying us any attention. "We straight."

Tony kept one hand on the table. He placed his other hand under the table. I opened my legs a little. He slipped his hand under my skirt and his fingers met my already wet pussy.

"Damn, baby. This for me?"

"For you, big daddy," I said, as the words purred off my lips.

Our eyes locked. I squirmed in my chair as he made my pussy talk back to him. The couple at the table next to us looked in our direction and smiled. I smiled back. The woman winked her eye.

"I can tell my pussy missed me," Tony said.

"Yesss, baby, it sure did," I responded.

"How much?" he asked.

I bit down on my bottom lip as I creamed on his fingers.

"Damn, baby," he said as he removed his fingers from under my skirt and then placed them in his mouth and sucked my juices off his fingers one by one. "You still taste as sweet as honey."

"And you still know how to make that pussy wet."

"I wish I could fuck you right now," Tony said.

KAYENNE

I eased my hand under the table. He grabbed it. "I just want to return the favor."

"My dick's rock hard. Let's talk so it'll go down. If I bust a nut now, it'll be messy. Trust me. I'll take care of it later when I'm by myself in my bunk."

I pouted. "I wish you would let me take care of it for you."

"Next time. Cause I know you're coming to see me again, and it won't take you three damn months."

I looked away. I felt a little guilty for taking so long to come see him. "No, it won't. I promise."

He sniffed his fingers. "Damn, baby. I might bust a nut right now."

We both laughed.

"Baby, why won't you tell me where the stuff is?" I tilted my head and blinked my eyes a few times.

"Mia, you got to trust me. I need that money for when I get out. If I tell you where it's at, it won't be nothing left when I get out."

"Yes, it will. Since you've been gone, I've gotten real good with money. I know how to budget and everything now."

"I'll believe that when I see it," he responded.

"I had no choice because the Feds confiscated all the money in our account. If it wasn't for the money I stashed in an account under my maiden name, I would have been homeless."

"I'm still pissed about that shit. I begged my lawyers to make sure they left you something, and he said there was nothing he could do."

"Bull shit. I never did like your lawyer." I could feel the anger building up, and I took a few deep breaths. "Enough of that, I got my own thing going on now. If everything works out, then I'm going to be on easy street."

"Mia, you better not be out there stripping."

"Come on now. You know me better than that."

"I'm just saying. If one of my boys tell me they saw you on a stripper pole, your ass is mine."

I laughed. He didn't. "Mia, I don't find that shit funny."

"Well, I do. Ain't shit you can do to me from in here. So, back to what I was saying. I got my own thing going on and things are finally looking up. How you think I was able to put a hundred on your books? Sure wasn't from that job I wear my feet out for everyday."

"I thought you got a bonus," Tony responded.

I leaned over and whispered, sharing with Tony some of the things I had going on.

"So, your girl is a businesswoman. She's doing her own thing." I leaned back in my chair proudly.

"I don't know if I want you doing what you doing, but I'm in here, and you got to do what you got to do."

What Tony didn't know, whether he approved or not, I was still going to get my hustle on. No approval from him was needed.

CHAPTER EIGHTEEN
China

I sat across from the bank manager, wondering why he was calling me into his office. This meeting was unplanned. He normally gave me a heads up when we were to have a meeting. His phone kept ringing, interrupting.

The palm of my hands started sweating. I wiped them on my skirt and clenched my fingers together as I impatiently waited.

"China, as you know we pride ourselves at this bank on excellence," Mr. Belk said.

"Yes, I know. That's the company's mantra."

"I've been watching you these last few weeks."

Oh. Shit. I looked behind me to see if the Feds were going to walk in the door with some handcuffs. I had to think of something to say and quick. "But . . ."

"Let me finish," he said, interrupting me. "I want to offer you a position as a Loan Officer. You've shown me in the short span that you've been back that you're a dedicated employee. You have a good track record from when you previously worked here. The customers rave about you."

I saw his lips moving and heard some of the things he said, but all I could concentrate on was the fact that there were no men in black suits or uniforms coming to arrest me. I blurted out, "Yes."

"So you'll take the position?" he asked.

"Yes, of course," I responded.

"Good. Now I want you to know that there may be nights where you'll have to work late."

"That won't be a problem," I assured Mr. Belk.

"It's settled. I'll have Kathy bring you the paperwork, and you can start your new position on Monday. I will need you to train your replacement on what to do once we hire someone."

"Will I not be doing the paperwork like I do now?" I asked.

"Sometimes. The person we hire to fill your position will be responsible for most of it."

"So when will you think that will be?" I asked.

"I'm going to call the employment agency today, so we can start interviewing candidates. You'll still enter some, but the bulk of your responsibility will be gathering the information. The clerk will be the one who will enter it into the computer."

"Oh okay. Then that works for me."

Gathering the information was even better. At first I thought that would put a damper on our operation but instead it wouldn't.

* * *

"Right there. Yes, that's it. That's itttt," I moaned as Chip pumped his nine inches of rock hard, thick dick in and out of me. He wasn't just packing weight—he knew how to use it.

Chip flipped me over, and now I was on top looking down into his handsome face. He positioned his body so my nipple was in his mouth as I rode him.

86

KAYENNE

We both couldn't seem to get enough of each other. I felt my pussy walls grip his dick and an orgasm so strong ripped through my body and we climaxed together. He fell back and I fell back on top of him. He kissed me lightly on the lips.

I could feel his heartbeat and he could feel mine. I could lie like this forever.

"Baby, I wish I could stay, but I got to go if I'm going to finish getting everything set up for your girl."

"I know. I just hate that we don't have more time together," I confessed.

The attraction between Chip and I had been there from the start, but we never acted on it because he was with Mia first. But last week when he stopped by, he caught me just getting out of the shower, and before either of us realized it, we were fucking right there on the stairway. Thankfully, he was smart enough to pull out a condom because the way I was feeling on that night, I would have fucked him raw and all.

I couldn't afford to be that careless with all of the deadly diseases out there, number one HIV, but that's how much in heat I was. It'd been awhile since I'd felt a man inside of me. Contrary to what some might think, I was faithful to my husband. Not once did I stray. He turned out to be the one that couldn't be trusted, not me.

Chip and I had been fucking almost every day since. It's like I couldn't get enough of his long, chocolate rod. I was a chocoholic and I loved it. I loved every inch of it.

"Can't it wait?" I asked, using one of my hands to stroke his dick.

"Ooh. China, you trying to start something again."

"No, I'm not," I responded, feigning innocence.

Soon I replaced my hand with my mouth. I looked up into his eyes as I took him in inch by inch. I could see the desire radiate from his eyes. He could barely contain himself as I licked and sucked on the head like it was a lollipop. I used my other hand and massaged his balls. His cum tasted sweet as I licked it up as it oozed out of the head.

"Damn baby, you got me hooked," Chip confessed.

I went to the bathroom and got a wet towel and cleaned myself up. When I returned to the room, I had to laugh. Chip wasn't going anywhere right now. He was fast asleep. That last round knocked him out. Wore me out too.

I heard his cell phone beep. He didn't bulge. I knew I shouldn't, but curiosity got the best of me. I had to know if he was messing with other women. I reached for his cell phone.

He grabbed my arm. "What are you doing?"

KAYENNE

CHAPTER NINETEEN
Trina

I'd been having a bad day all day. I woke up late. Had to rush and drop the kids off to school so they wouldn't be marked as tardy. I got to work late and here it was three in the afternoon and I was sitting on the side of West 70th Street with a flat tire. Not one person had stopped to help.

A police officer who passed me a few minutes ago did an illegal U-turn and parked directly behind my car. He turned on his flashing lights without the siren. I hoped he wasn't trying to give me a ticket. All I needed was my flat to be changed.

The door opened and the finest man I'd ever seen stepped out. I don't know if it was the uniform, or if he just had one of those bodies. As he neared me, I forgot all about my tire.

He called out to me several times before I responded, "Yeah. My tire's flat."

"I can see that. Do you have help on the way?"

"No." I pouted, glancing at his badge. "Officer Warner."

"If you have a jack and a spare, I can change it," he offered.

SWIPE

I opened the trunk and watched him with his bulging muscles change my flat.

"Thank you, Officer Warner," I said.

"Call me Dale," he said as he placed my torn up tire in my trunk and closed it.

"Dale, thank you. If it hadn't been for you, I would still be trying to figure out how to get this tire changed."

"I can teach you how to change your tire so you won't have to depend on anybody else. Well anybody, if I'm not around." He smiled, showcasing some deep dimples.

"Sure. When do you want to teach me?" I asked.

"I'm off tomorrow. What about you?"

"I get off at three but have to pick up my kids from school, so what about five?"

"Five it is," he responded.

I walked to get in my car.

He called out, "You didn't tell me your name or number. So how am I going to reach you?"

"You got my license plate number. Figure it out." I twisted and put a little bounce in my big booty as I continued to walk to my car.

I slid in the driver's seat and then glanced in my rearview mirror. Dale was staring at the car, or I guess my booty hypnotized him. I blew my horn as I eased out into traffic. He got back in his patrol car and didn't come in my direction. Instead he turned and drove the opposite way.

The next day, I wasn't surprised to see him standing on the other side of my door.

"Dale, so you figured out how to find me?" I said.

KAYENNE

He wasn't wearing a police uniform. Instead he was dressed in a New Orleans Saints T-shirt and a pair of blue jeans. His muscles were ripped. From the look of his fit and muscular body, he made the uniform—the uniform did not make him.

"Ms. Katrina, are you ready for your lesson?"

"It's Trina, and I will be after I make sure these kids have eaten their food. Come on in."

I moved to the side as he entered.

"You got your place fixed up real nice," he said.

"Thanks. Just because I live in the hood doesn't mean I don't like to live nice," I responded.

"Trina." He chuckled. "No need for attitude. I came to help, remember?"

"Mama, who is that?" Xavier walked in and said.

"Boy, go back in the kitchen and sit down and eat."

"But Mama, who is that?"

"That's okay, Trina. I'm Dale and who are you?" Dale reached his hand out to Xavier.

Xavier hesitated at first, but then shook Dale's hand. "People call me X." Xavier folded his arms.

"Well, X, I'm here to teach your mama how to change a flat tire. If you like, I can show you too."

"Cool. Mama, can I watch? Please," he said. Xavier knew I couldn't resist his big puppy dog eyes.

"Fine, finish eating and then you can watch."

I led Dale to the sofa. "Before you ask, I have three kids. They are triplets."

"Wow. Where's their dad?" he asked.

"He got killed. So they're my full responsibility."

"Triplets though. You're the first person I've met with triplets. I know some people with twins or three kids, but triplets. You're the first."

"I guess you regret coming over to give me that lesson now, don't you?"

"No. Should I?"

"Usually when I tell guys that, they run the other way."

"I'm not like other guys."

"How are you different?"

"If you give me some time, I will show you." He licked his lips.

I bit my bottom lip. "Uhhh. I got to check on the kids. I'll be right back."

I don't think I exhaled until I was out of his sight.

Zahara asked, "You okay, Mama?"

I had to pull myself together and quick. "Yes, baby. Mama just needed to catch her breath. Y'all through eating?"

"Yes, ma'am."

"Za and Yasmin, wash up. X is about to help me with something."

"You lucky you a boy and don't have to wash dishes," Zahara said to her brother.

"I do wash dishes, don't I Mama?" Xavier said.

"Za, you know he does. Now leave him alone."

It took Dale almost an hour to teach me how to change a tire. I did feel a little more confident that I could change one if I got a flat again though.

"X, go in the house."

"Bye, Mr. Dale," Xavier said.

"Bye, lil' man," he responded. He looked at me. "I haven't met your daughters yet, but your little guy is so polite."

"You need to catch him on another day. He's always messing with his sisters. It probably won't be long before one of them runs out here screaming or crying because they are always getting into a fight, especially my two girls."

Dale reached for my hand. I placed it in his. He walked me to the door. "I hope you'll let me take you out sometime."

"I can't always get a babysitter, so you might want to reconsider."

"I can pick up something for us and your kids and bring it over. We can have movie night right here."

"I would love that."

"I'm off Saturday, so how about Saturday night?" he asked.

"Saturday works for me," I responded.

"Ms. Trina, I will see you on Saturday."

"It's a date."

I watched Dale get in his car and drive off. For the first time in a long time I actually looked forward to something.

CHAPTER TWENTY
Mia

I'd been spending the last few days at what we called the trap house. It was a small two-bedroom house big enough to house some of our merchandise sitting right in the heart of the Cedar Grove neighborhood. We weren't selling drugs, but we were selling merchandise gained by illegal means. We'd only been officially taking orders for a week and already business was booming. I met with China and Chip to devise a system that would work for all of us. All cell phones had to be checked in at the door before entering. We didn't need anyone snapping pictures and posting anything on Facebook or Instagram.

The girls that Chip got to work with me were a few years younger. I don't know if I trusted them, but they seemed to follow directions well. They brought in the orders. I did the research and placed the orders and had the items sent to various post offices around the city. Either China, Trina, or I would go pick up the packages.

Once the items were in, the girls were contacted and they came to pick up the items and distributed to the person who bought it. They gave me the money and I gave them a small portion. There was twenty-four hour security, just in case someone got stupid and thought they could raid our spot. The remainder of the money was split evenly among the four of us. I didn't really want to give Chip twenty-five percent, but he did do a lot of work for us and brought in the girls, so I reluctantly gave in to that agreement.

I was finding it harder and harder to work around Chip. He always smelled good. He wore the same kind of cologne Tony used to wear. I loved Tony, but I needed the feel of a man. The only thing stopping me from approaching Chip was the fact that Tony could probably forgive me for sleeping with any other man, except Chip. If it wasn't for that, I would be jumping on that. I was surprised Chip never tried to come on to me. At first, he used to flirt with me, but a few weeks ago, the flirting stopped. I guess Chip had finally gotten over me. It took him seven years to do so, but oh well. I guess it's a good thing, because I didn't need that kind of static.

One of my two cell phones rang. I had to figure out which one because they both were in the bottom of my purse.

It was the business phone. "Hello," I said. No answer, just heavy breathing. I hung up. The phone rang again. The number was blocked. This time I let the call go to voice mail.

I got my other phone out of my purse and dialed China's throwaway phone. She didn't answer but called me back a few minutes later.

"What's up?" she asked.

"I'm getting hang up calls from an unknown number. Time to get a new phone."

"I'll send Chip to drop it off. I don't need to be seen in the area."

"That's fine. I wouldn't mind seeing that fine Chip anyway."

"What did you say?" she asked, sounding like she had an attitude when she said it.

"Nothing. Just send Chip with the phone. I cut the other one off and removed the battery."

"On second thought, why don't you close down shop. Pick up Trina and y'all meet me and Chip at my place."

"China, now don't take what I'm about to say wrong, but why we always got to come out there? What's wrong with you coming out this way sometimes?"

"Because this is the one place I know that is one hundred percent secure. Out here we don't have to worry about anyone overhearing us. Don't have to worry about any cameras. It's safe and secure."

China had a point. Although I still had my personal beef with her, I had to give her credit for starting this lucrative business. We were all getting paid and paid well without investing any of our own money.

"I'll call Trina and see if she can get away. You keep forgetting she can't just go somewhere. She's got those kids."

"I'm sure she can afford to pay a babysitter now," China responded, right before hanging up.

Two hours later, Trina and I were pulling up beside Chip's SUV in China's driveway.

"I see Chip's already here," I said as I exited the car.

Trina rang the doorbell. We waited and waited.

"What's taking her so long? She's the one who wanted to meet up," I said.

"I don't know," Trina said. "But she needs to hurry up because I got to pee."

China finally opened the door. She had her hair pulled back in a ponytail and a robe wrapped around her.

"'Bout time. I got to pee," Trina said, as she rushed past China and headed straight to one of her downstairs bathrooms.

I walked in casually. China seemed to have a special glow about herself.

"Chip's in the den. I'll meet y'all there. Let me go finish getting dressed."

Chip was watching television when I entered. He lowered the volume when he saw me. He got up and greeted me with a hug.

"What's up, Mia?"

"Nothing much. What's been going on with you? We need to catch up."

He sat back down and I sat next to him. He responded, "I'm just living life, baby girl. Just living life."

"You seeing anybody?" I asked.

"Dang girl, you sure are nosy." He picked up the remote and started changing channels.

"I'm just making small talk." I crossed my legs and my skirt eased up.

He shifted his body in the other direction.

"What I do in my personal life ain't got nothing to do with you, but to answer your question, I am seeing somebody."

"Anybody I know?" I asked.

SWIPE

Trina walked in. "I almost got lost. This house is so big."

Trina's timing couldn't be more off. I was just about to get an answer from Chip. Looking at him now made me want to reconsider trying to push up on him. If I tried, I knew he wouldn't be able to resist.

Chip and Trina talked about the kids while I pretended to be engrossed in the movie being shown on TV.

China walked in looking fresh with her pink jogging suit on. She walked near Chip. He moved his leg, and then she rudely plopped her behind in between Chip and me. I moved over to the right to give her more room. If I hadn't, we would have been sitting on the couch like a can of sardines.

Inside I was like, "What the fuck!" But I kept the comment to myself.

KAYENNE

CHAPTER TWENTY-ONE
China

When I walked in the den and saw Mia sitting all up under Chip, I knew I had to break that up, so neither one of them would get any ideas of rekindling their teenage love affair. I could tell Mia was a little uncomfortable when I sat between the two of them, but I didn't care. Chip looked at me because he knew exactly why I did what I did. He and I would be having our own private conversation later. Believe that.

"Ladies, good to see you both. Any updates y'all want to give me?" I asked.

Trina sat in the chair across from the couch, so I had direct eye contact with her. I couldn't see Mia's facial expression because I failed to look in her direction.

Trina said, "It's been hectic on the job lately, so I haven't been able to get that many cards."

I was disappointed in that. If Trina couldn't hold up her end, then we would have to rethink her cut. We were friends, but business was business.

I finally looked over at Mia. "What about you? You mentioned some hang up calls. You notice any suspicious vehicles driving around the area?"

Mia shifted in her seat. "Nothing out of the ordinary. I make sure I have on a semi-disguise when

I go to the trap house anyway. I still have the fake plates on my car, so my car can't be traced back to me like you told me."

"Just checking. We got a good thing going here, ladies." I looked at Chip. "And gentleman. Let's not fuck it up."

Mia said, "I'm thinking about quitting my job at the store because fulfilling these orders is taking up a lot of my time."

"But we need the credit card information in order to continue to do what we're doing," Trina said.

"You just worry about what you got going on and I'll worry about Mia," Mia responded.

Trina held up her middle finger.

"Ladies. Ladies. No need for that," I said, interfering.

Mia said, "The only other option is for me to cut back on my hours because it is becoming too much."

"Let me think about it and we can revisit this later."

"What's there to think about?" Mia asked. "If I decide to quit, that's my prerogative."

This bitch was going to make me slap her. I clenched my fists, closed my eyes and counted to three to calm myself. "Fine, Mia. You just let us know what you decide."

"Chip, everything okay on your end?" Mia asked.

"Everything is fine," he responded bluntly.

"You sure about that? Why am I getting hang ups?" Mia asked.

Chip didn't like being questioned about his end of the operation. "Mia, I don't know. You tell me. For all we know, you and your man might have some side deals going on."

Mia stood up. She put her hand on her hip and started slinging her long black weave. "Look a here. Tony don't know shit about this." She used her hand to illustrate. "And even if he did, so fucking what!"

I grabbed Mia by the hand. "Calm down. Both of y'all. The hang up calls could be anybody, so chill out."

Chip clenched his jaw. "Fuck that, China. This trick trying to say I'm not handling my side of things, and I ain't got time for that."

"Trick? Bitch ass nigga, I got your trick!" Mia looked fighting mad.

I stood up because there was no way I was going to let her hit my man. Chip remained seated.

"Mia, sit your ass down." We looked each other square in the eyes.

Trina said, "Mia, come on now. Chill."

Mia reluctantly sat down. I remained standing, but then walked near the television so everyone could see me.

"We can't be having no fighting if this operation is to remain a success. If anyone has any beef with anyone, let us put it all out on the table and clear the air."

It got quiet in the room.

"Everybody cool with everybody?" I asked as I paced the floor in front of the television.

Mia looked up at me and sighed out loud. I stared at her. "Mia, if you got something to say. Say it now or forever hold your peace."

SWIPE

She leaned back in her seat. "Yeah, I got something to say. Why you walking around here acting like you everyone's boss?"

"Because one, this was my idea. I didn't have to come to none of y'all. I could have easily worked directly with Chip and cut y'all both out, but I didn't. I wanted to share this with my girls."

"Bitch, please. You needed us, so don't even front," Mia responded.

"I'll admit things wouldn't be going like they are going if it wasn't for y'all, but with any organization there has to be a lead. And again, since it was my idea, I took the lead role. Anything else?"

Mia and I had a staring match. Chip and Trina both remained quiet.

"And another thing. When did you and Chip start fucking?" Mia said.

"Excuse me," I responded. She caught me totally off guard with that question.

"You heard me. When did y'all start fucking?"

Chip answered for me. "Mia, what goes on between me and China is none of your fucking business."

"See, I knew it. When I hugged Chip, I smelled the perfume that you wear. He just confirmed it."

Mia was getting on my nerves. So what if Chip and I had something going on. Her time with him was history. She needed to get over it and stay the hell out of my business. If I didn't need her to be the go between in our operation, I would kick her out of my house.

"Look, Mia. As Chip said, what we got going on or not, is none of your business. The only business you should be concerned with is making sure you handle those orders."

Trina said, "This is better than any of my reality shows. Just call y'all The Real Girls in the Hood." She laughed.

"Look around, baby. This is not the hood," I said.

"You might not be in the hood, but you sure got some hood tendencies. Carry on," Trina said as she leaned back in her chair and looked at me and then Mia.

"Fuck both of y'all bitches. I'm not going to take too many more of these disrespectful comments up in my house."

"I don't need this shit," Mia said. "Come on, Trina. Let's get out of here."

Chip stood up. "All of y'all shut the fuck up. Mia, sit your ass down. "

Mia huffed and puffed, but she sat down.

CHAPTER TWENTY-TWO
Trina

When Chip got up, I remained seated.

Chip looked at all of us. "You all are supposed to be friends, but the way y'all going back and forth, I can't tell."

"Mia, obviously, you're still upset at China, but you need to get over that shit. You can't fault her for trying to do better for herself. Shit, you left the hood when that nigga of yours bought you a house."

Mia rolled her eyes.

"China, you need to check yourself too. I can understand where Mia's coming from. I don't care where you go in life, you should never forget your peeps."

China folded her arms and tapped her foot. "I didn't forget nobody."

"Well, when you don't call or come by to see anyone, what do you call that?" Mia blurted out.

"I didn't want to come back to the neighborhood because I was raped there. Happy now?" China blurted out and tears started flowing down her cheeks.

I rarely saw China cry. Chip wrapped his arms around her and rocked her back and forth.

Mia looked at me and I looked at her. We were both speechless.

China moved. Chip dropped his arm from around her.

KAYENNE

I looked up at China. "Sorry, we didn't know."

"Why didn't you tell us? We would have been there for you," Mia said. She no longer had anger or an attitude in her voice when she talked to China.

"Because I was ashamed. It happened one night when I was walking home from Mia's house."

Mia blinked her eyes a few times. She took over the conversation from China. "You didn't come to school for a few days. When you did come to school you barely said anything. That's when you told us you had decided that you were going to LSU."

"Yes. I wanted to get as far away as possible. When I got the scholarship that was my opportunity."

I asked, "What happened to the man who raped you?"

Chip answered instead of China. "He's six feet under. China wasn't his only victim."

"Glad to see the scum got what was coming to him," I said. I couldn't even imagine going through what China went through. If anyone put their hands on one of my girls I would kill them too.

Mia stood up and walked over to China. "I'm sorry. I'm sorry for what you went through, and I'm sorry for acting the way I have with you."

China wiped the tears from her face with the tissue Chip had handed to her. "There's nothing to be sorry for. Maybe if I would have told y'all, you would have understood."

"And y'all wouldn't be going at each other like this," Chip added. "Now can you two hug and make up so we can get back to talking about how to make this money?"

We all chuckled.

China said, "Group hug?"

I got up and joined in on the group hug.

Chip stood back and watched. "You females can fight one minute and be all back friendly the next. I'll never understand y'all."

"Whatever, dude. You can join in the hug," I said.

"Thought you'd never ask." Chip walked up behind us and hugged us.

We laughed and then all took a seat back in our original positions. The rest of the evening went smooth.

Mia drove me back home. "You think her and Chip got something going on?"

"If they do, they grown."

"But Chip was mine first."

"Mia, I thought things were cool between you and China now."

"They are, but come on. Out of all of the men out there, China had to pick Chip. Chip was my first."

"You're married now, so that shouldn't even be an issue."

"What about the girl code?"

"What about it? You moved on. Chip's on the open market. Besides, that was years ago. You left Chip to be with Tony, remember?"

"I know, but still . . . Chip was my first, and now him and China are fucking?"

"You really don't know if that's true anyway, so why trip over it?" I said while trying to find my house keys in my purse.

"Neither one denied it. Besides, I smelled her perfume and his breath smelled like pussy."

I laughed. "Then you was too damn close to Chip if you smelled all of that."

"I'm just saying. That nigga didn't gargle or nothing after eating her pussy. He could have at least done that."

"If they getting their swerve on, let them. They both deserve to be happy."

"At my expense?" she asked as she pulled up in front of my house.

"Of course, I'm not saying that. What I'm saying is . . . if they fucking, so what. That ain't got shit to do with you."

"I guess you right, but I still don't like it," Mia said.

"I got a man I got to get ready for, so I will see you later." I unbuckled my seat belt.

Mia grabbed my arm. "Hold up. When did this happen? I hope it ain't Ray Ray's stupid behind."

"No. It's a new guy."

"Details. Why is this the first time I'm hearing about him?"

I glanced at the clock on my cell phone. "I'll have to tell you about him later. He'll be over here in less than an hour, and I need to go freshen up."

"So no wonder you didn't worry about getting the kids tonight, because your ass got a date."

"You know it." Without waiting for Mia to comment, I jumped out the car and went inside my house. Officer Dale Warner was coming over, and I had some plans for him and hopefully they would involve his handcuffs.

SWIPE

CHAPTER TWENTY-THREE
Mia

Trina didn't understand my feelings concerning Chip. Chip was my first, so what we had would always be special. China knew he was my first, so although we squashed our old beef of her abandoning us, her friends, I still wasn't too keen on the idea of her hooking up with Chip.

I got home and took a long bubble bath. Every time I closed my eyes I imagined Chip and China fucking. I needed to quit because Trina was right. I have a husband, an absent husband, but a husband nevertheless.

The loud noise at my door woke me up. I'd drifted off to sleep in the tub. I dried off quickly and grabbed my robe and went to look out my peephole.

"I hope you got my money," I said as soon as I unlocked the door and opened it.

Casper stood there with his short self, looking as good as ever with a huge smile on his face. "Can I come in?"

"Come on." I was lonely and horny, and if he had my money I was going to fulfill one of those needs tonight.

He pulled out a wad of money and handed it to me. I counted it. "With interest I see. You can stay."

"I got to run, but I just wanted to give you yours."

I let my robe slip off. "No, you ain't going nowhere."

Casper licked his lips. "What I had going on can wait."

"That's what I thought."

Little man was strong. He picked me up and carried me to my bedroom. He propped my legs open and dived right in with his tongue devouring me like he was starving. I obliged him by giving him what he wanted.

He pulled off his clothes. While he was doing that, I got a condom from the nightstand near my bed. I eased it on his long curved dick.

"Lay down," I commanded.

He did what he was told.

I eased down on him and rode him like a prized stallion. Going up and down and round and round. He moaned out in pleasure. It didn't take long for either one of us to reach the peak. That was just what I needed to get me through the night.

Casper dozed off. I hit him on the arm. "Wake up. You got to go. Besides, I thought you had somewhere you needed to be."

"They can wait," he said, closing his eyes.

"Casper, get up."

"Come on, Mia."

"No. You came over to drop off the money. Now it's time for you to go."

Casper got up and put on his clothes. "So you just used me?"

SWIPE

"No. If I was using you, then you would be hurt. But the way you were screaming a few minutes ago, you got nothing but pleasure out of what I did to you."

"I should be mad, but I ain't mad at you." He pulled me into an embrace. His head rested on top of my breasts. He looked up at me. "So when can we hook up again?"

"I'll call you," I responded as I pulled him toward the front door.

"I'm going to be waiting on that call," Casper said as he got a good feel of my butt before walking out the door.

I shut and locked the door behind him. Casper would be a ghost in my life, because I'd just decided I was moving. I was getting enough money, so it was time for me to move out of the neighborhood. It was time for me to not only upgrade my surroundings but the type of men I messed with.

The phone rang. I saw the prison number on the display. Tony's voice rang from the other end after the recording did its spiel.

"You know if I was on the street, I would fuck you up right about now," he yelled from the other end.

"What are you talking about?" I asked.

"One of my boys told me you've been fucking with Chip. If that's true, there's going to be hell to pay."

"First of all, don't come calling me with no bullshit you heard. If you want to know something about what I got going on, you need to call me and show some motherfuckin' respect."

"Respect? Mia, you trying me. You better start explaining yourself." I could imagine the veins about to pop out of his head and the spit on his mouth because when he got upset that's how he appeared.

"I ain't got shit going on with Chip. If your so-called reporter want to go back and report something they need to get the story straight."

"I heard you was riding around town with that nigga. Ain't no woman of mine got any business with another man. You fucking him? Huh? Tell me the truth."

"No, I'm not fucking him," I responded. That was the truth. He didn't need to know that I'd been sleeping with other men. I took on the same policy as men. 'Don't ask don't tell.'

"Then why you riding around with him? Huh, Mia, tell me that!"

"I told you when I saw you, that I got my own business."

"So you in bed with Chip?"

"Chip gave me a ride, so what? You not here to do it."

"Mia, you pushing me. Don't go there."

"All you need to know is that I'm not f-u-c-k-i-n-g Chip. Is that understood?"

"Then I don't want to hear nothing else about that nigga. If I do, not only am I going to fuck him up, you and I will have beef."

It was on the tip of my tongue to tell Tony to screw himself, but I refrained from doing it. He then tried to switch gears in the conversation and sounded disappointed when I didn't want to get all lovey dovey with him.

"Baby, you forgive me, right?"

SWIPE

"Yeah, whatever, Tony. Look, time's 'bout to run out anyway. Love you."

He responded, "I love you too, baby girl."

The phone disconnected and it was for the best. I curled up under the covers. I didn't know how much longer I could take this. Being married to someone incarcerated was not how I planned on living out my life. I'm only twenty-three. When Tony got imprisoned, it seemed like I got imprisoned too.

KAYENNE

CHAPTER TWENTY-FOUR
China

"Oooh, Chip. Oohhh," I screamed out as Chip's mouth held on to my clit and had me screaming out with pleasure.

With his lips glistening with my juices, he eased up on top of me and entered me. Our bodies were in sync as the bed rocked.

"I love you, baby," Chip said as he dug deeper and deeper.

I moaned out in pleasure. We climaxed together and fell into each other's arms. He brushed my hair from in front of my eyes.

"Did you hear me?" he asked.

"I heard you, and my neighbors down the street probably heard me," I joked.

"Ha. Ha. I'm talking about when I said I love you. I mean that, you know."

"Of course you love me when we're sexing."

"I care about you. I love you and it's not about the sex. Well, correction, the sex is part of it, but I love you, China. Your husband was a fool for cheating on you. Let me love you like you should be loved."

I looked down. I wasn't expecting this. I had feelings for Chip, but love . . . I wasn't too sure if that was how I would describe those feelings. Lust, most definitely, because his body was just as fine as that actor Omari Hardwick, but love . . . After Gerry, did I really want to tread down that road again?

"China, did you hear me?" he asked again.

"Are you sure?" I asked, trying to bide myself some time as I thought of a response to his revelation.

"If you give me the chance, I'll show you," he said as he planted a kiss on my forehead.

I didn't want to hurt Chip, but I needed time to digest all of this. "Chip, I care about you. You know that. But I just got a divorce. I don't know if I should be jumping into something serious right away."

"I'm okay to fuck, but not love. Is that what you're saying?" Chip shifted his body and sat up. My body slid down on the bed. I then sat up.

"No. You're taking it all wrong. I care. I really do. I just don't want to hurt you. I don't want you to hurt me. We got to think about how Mia will feel about all of this. So many things we got to think about."

Chip got up. "I know what I want and who I want. I don't have to think about shit. You, on the other hand, might need some time to think about what you really want. Because I love you, I'm going to give you all of the time you need." He began putting on his clothes.

"Where are you going?"

"I'm going home. You can start your thinking process tonight."

"But Chip, it's late. Come on back to bed."

He leaned across the bed and gave me a quick peck on the lips. "Come lock up."

Chip walked out the door. Without bothering to put on a robe, I followed him. He continued going down the stairs. He went to the living room to look for his keys. I stood in front of the front door blocking it.

"Come on, China. Move now."

"No. I don't want you to go." I batted my eyes.

"It's best that I do. I want you to figure out what you want. If it's not me, my feelings will be hurt, but we'll still be cool."

"I do want you. Is that what you want to hear?" I said, wrapping my arms around his neck.

He eased my arm from around his neck, picked me up, and moved me to the side. "I want to hear you say you love me. Good night, China."

Chip kissed me again. I melted on the spot. He walked out of the house, closing the door behind him.

I think I was in love with Chip but I was scared. What if he ended up like every other man I'd been with? I know I was only twenty-three, but I'd seen enough heartache to last me a lifetime. I wasn't too sure I wanted to chance it again.

I held my hand on the doorknob, closed my eyes and then jerked it open, naked body and all.

Chip stood in front of the door.

"I thought you were gone," I said.

He came back inside, shielding me with his body. "You need to put some clothes on if you're going to open your door like that." He closed the door and locked it.

"I would have run down the street to catch you if you hadn't been standing there," I said.

He laughed. "I would have liked to have seen that."

"I'm sure you would." I laughed too.

SWIPE

He grabbed my hand and kissed it. "So what were you coming after me for?"

"Chip, I'm scared. I'm scared if I love you, that you will hurt me just like everyone else."

His hand wiped the lone tear that fell from my eye. "You'll never have to worry about me hurting you. I love you. I'm here for you. Just trust me, baby. That's all I ask."

"I don't know. My heart can't take any more heartbreak."

Chip tilted my head back, so he was looking directly into my eyes. "I can promise you two things. Number one, that I love you and there's nothing I wouldn't do to show you. Number two, I will never hurt you intentionally. My word is my bond."

I hesitated before responding, "Pinky swear promise."

"Huh?"

"When I was little, me and my friends would make a pinky swear promise whenever we promised each other something."

"I'll do a cross my heart and hope to die promise if it'll get you to admit the feelings you have for me," Chip responded.

I looked up in Chip's eyes and recited the three words he'd been wanting to hear, "I love you."

"Now was that so hard?"

"No. In fact, it felt liberating."

"Show your man how much you love him," he commanded.

Chip thought he was in control. I needed to show him who was really the captain of this ship.

KAYENNE

CHAPTER TWENTY-FIVE
Trina

My romantic evening with Dale was a bust. We were so close to making out when his cell phone rang. He received an emergency call and had to go help one of his fellow officers. But it didn't stop him from returning this morning for a big hearty breakfast that I promised to make.

I watched him lick his lips after devouring my thick brown pancakes.

"What time do you go to work?" he asked.

"I'm off."

"I don't go in until three, so looks like we have some time to talk."

I got up and walked around to where he sat. I wrapped my arm around his neck and kissed him on the cheek. "Talking is the last thing I want to do."

Ten minutes later, we were tearing each other's clothes off.

"I've been wanting you from the first time I saw you," he said as he breathed heavily.

"Me too," I responded as I removed another item.

Both of us were now down to our underwear. I crawled up on the bed. Dale followed me. He pushed his tongue down my throat. His hands roamed across my body. With one hand, he unsnapped my bra and continued to kiss me as he eased the straps off my shoulders. He rubbed my nipples with one hand, but soon placed his lips where his hand had been. My body arched. Moans seeped out. I could feel myself getting wetter and wetter.

He used his free hand and played with my clit as he sucked on each nipple. He planted kisses all down my chest. By the time his lips found my core, my back was perfectly arched.

Dale dipped his tongue in and out of my clit while using his fingers to go in and out of my pussy. He had me so wet I could hear the slushing sound.

I creamed all in his mouth.

"Dale, I need you inside of me now."

"I'm about to give it to you."

He reached into his wallet and took out a condom. He placed it over his fully erect dick and eased it inside of my wet pussy walls. We both "oohed" and "aahed" as our bodies connected. I thought Ray Ray knew how to work the pussy. Dale showed me he was a master at it because he had the pussy talking back to him as my legs shivered.

"Let me see that ass clap," he said, flipping me over and hitting it from the back.

I gave him just what he wanted. My ass cheeks clapped together each time he pumped in and out. He reached in front of me and grabbed my breasts. He let out a huge load into his condom, and we both fell down on the bed with him on top of my back.

We lay there in that position until both of our heart rates returned to normal. He rolled off me. I led him into the bathroom and turned on the shower. We took turns washing each other. He pinned me up against the wall in the shower. I wrapped one of my legs around his waist as he penetrated me again. We made love as the water hit his back and splashed in my face. I closed my eyes and held on for dear life as we both climaxed together. I didn't even think about a condom until I felt his hot wet sperm inside me.

We finished bathing. After dressing, Dale drove out to the lake. We walked around, holding hands and talking.

"I know I'm sort of doing things backward, but I'm not seeing anyone else and you're not seeing anyone else. Let's see if we can work something out," he said.

So there would be no misunderstandings, I asked, "So you and me are like girlfriend and boyfriend . . . meaning we shouldn't be fucking with nobody else but each other, right?"

"Yeah. That's exactly what I'm saying." He hugged me and then grabbed the bottom of my butt and lifted me up. "I don't want nobody else getting a hold of this."

"Dale, put me down." I playfully hit him.

He put me down and we kissed.

When he dropped me off back at home, Mia's car was parked outside.

"I forgot I was supposed to be meeting my girl. Let me get rid of her, and then we can continue to hang out," I said.

He looked at his watch. "I need to go home and change and get ready for my shift anyway. I'll call you later."

I reached for the latch on the door.

"Aren't you forgetting something?" he asked as I opened the door.

"Oh, yeah." I leaned over and kissed him. He dipped his tongue inside my mouth. I could feel moisture between my legs just from his kiss.

"Damn, baby. You're going to make me call in sick," he said as I pulled away.

"Just call me."

"I get off around midnight. I might need to swing through."

"Sounds good to me. The kids should be sleep and we can do our thing."

We said our final good-byes. I watched him pull off. When I turned to walk toward the door, Mia was now standing outside of her car.

"So that's the mystery man. He's a cutie," Mia said.

"Yes, he is." Mia followed me inside. "Excuse the mess. I haven't had time to clean up."

"Obviously. You've been too busy getting your swerve on."

"Girl, let me tell you. He got a big ass dick and knows exactly what to do with it."

"He must do because you walking around here with a big ol' smile on your face," Mia said.

"As long as he keeps a smile on my face, I'll be keeping him around. Besides, he don't come with the type of drama Ray Ray was bringing."

"So I dropped by to pick up that list of stuff you wanted me to order."

I went to my room and found the list I'd written down. I returned and handed it to her. "Don't tell China about this because she would have a fit."

"It's not her business. The money we make from these sales, we'll just split between the two of us. Her and Chip don't have to know anything about this thing here."

"Cool. I just wanted to make sure," I responded. "One of my coworkers was asking me about ordering her some stuff. She'd heard through the grapevine that she could place orders and pay half the price for merchandise. I pretended like I didn't know what she was talking about."

"Glad you played it like that. You don't need to be tied to it at all."

"I told the co-worker to keep it on the low-low."

"Hopefully, they will. Now tell me about this dude you dating. I need some details. If I can't be happy, somebody in my circle needs to be."

CHAPTER TWENTY-SIX
Mia

I felt like a single woman with no place to go, so I plopped down on Trina's couch and waited for her to tell me about her new man.

She sat on the other end of the couch. With a huge smile on her face she recounted their day. "Just thinking about it makes my legs shake," she said.

"He got you hooked already."

"He had me hooked from the moment I saw him get out of his car."

"How did you meet?"

"Maybe we shouldn't talk about that," Trina said, looking off.

"Spit it out. You told me what y'all did in the bedroom, surely you can tell me about how y'all met."

"Promise me you won't get mad."

"Don't tell me he's married like that asshole Ray Ray."

"No. He's not married. He's a cop."

I blinked my eyes a few times. "A what?"

"He's a cop. We met when he stopped to help me change my flat tire."

I looked at her in disbelief. "You got to be kidding me. Trina, have you lost your mind? You got all of this stolen stuff in here. In fact, we're sitting on one of the items and you're screwing a cop."

"Calm down," Trina said.

"Calm! You sleeping with the enemy and I'm supposed to be calm."

"Dale and I don't talk about his job, nor do I talk about what I do when we're together."

"The relationship is new. Eventually, he will be divulging some information and you know you. You can't hold water. That's why if I have a secret I don't want no one else to know, I don't tell your ass."

"I do keep secrets. I didn't tell Tony you've been screwing other men."

"Bitch, you better not tell Tony anything. In fact, if Tony calls you again, don't accept his phone call. He shouldn't be calling you anyway trying to reach me. If I don't answer, that means I'm busy."

"Fine. I ain't trying to get in the middle of what y'all got going on."

"But back to you and this cop. You need to end it. The closer y'all get, the harder it's going to be for you, so you might as well end it now."

"The kids like him too. What am I supposed to tell them?"

"I don't know. All I know is you need to tell the cop you don't think things will work out between y'all. That you need to concentrate on you and your kids and don't have time for a man or something. You'll think of something."

Trina's cell phone beeped. She picked it up off the table and read it. "That was him letting me know he was at home."

"So when you going to do it?" I asked.

SWIPE

"I never agreed to doing anything," Trina responded.

"Fine. Do what you want. But if this shit blows up in your face, keep my name out of it."

"I'm not telling Dale anything about what we got going on, so you don't have anything to worry about."

"I wonder what China would have to say about this?"

Trina's eyes got dark. "China don't need to know anything about Dale. Understood?"

I threw my hand up in the air. "Do what you want to. You and your cop friend and China and Chip can have one big huge love fest for all I care."

"Do I sense a tone of jealousy?" Trina asked.

I poked out my lips. "Whatever."

"That's it! You're jealous that I may have found someone that I can be with for a long time. Someone who's not about that life. Who cares about me and my kids."

I shook my head back and forth. *Yada Yada Yada*, I said in my head as Trina blurted out all the reasons she thought I was jealous.

I laughed at the end of her rant.

"First of all, I'm not jealous of you or China. So let's get that straight."

"I sho' can't tell," Trina responded.

"Secondly, I'm just trying to save you future heartache. Cops only want girls like us to fuck. They don't want to be in a relationship."

Trina started rolling her neck. "Newsflash. Dale has asked me to be his girl, so yes, he wants me more than just for the booty."

"So he says," I responded.

KAYENNE

"Hater. The color don't look good on you."

I ran my hand from my shoulder to my knee. "With a body like mine, I don't need to hate."

"I think when you find your own man, you won't be so concerned about who's in my bed."

"Girl, I ain't got time for this foolishness. I got the list. I told you what I think and I'm out of here." I left Trina sitting on her couch.

CHAPTER TWENTY-SEVEN
China

It's been three months since Operation Make that Money started. Everything was going smoothly. The girls continued to get the credit cards and Chip continued to do his part. We had more accessible cash due to Chip's girls selling items directly to the consumers.

I used my cell phone to log into my bank account to check my balance. My bank account was looking real nice. So nice, that I would be able to hire another lawyer so I could see about getting my alimony increased.

After I put the phone in my pocket, I turned and faced the three most important people in my life right now.

"Glad you all could be here."

"Don't front. We know Chip practically lives here now," Mia blurted out.

I didn't have time for Mia and her attitude. Besides, Chip and I had dinner plans and it didn't include a third party, so the sooner I finished saying what I had to say, the sooner he and I could be on the way to the casino.

KAYENNE

Chip held a tray with flutes filled with champagne. Each person took a glass. He placed the tray down on the table in front of me.

"Things have been great. Teamwork is what got us here, so we must continue to work together."

I held up my glass and they all stood up and clinked glasses. I took a sip out of my flute. "It's been three months. I want to make sure everybody is saving up something because you know we can't keep doing this for too much longer. I suggest we do it for another three months and just chill."

"I don't see why not?" Mia said. "If we were going to get caught, it would have happened by now."

"We've all made some good money from this thing. I agree with China about everything but one," Chip said.

"What's that?" I asked.

"I think we need to end it now. The word is out on the streets, and you never know who talks to who. We had a good run with things. End it now. I got a nice little nest egg saved up. You got some, Trina? Mia?"

Mia said, "I'm doing all right. I could always use more."

Trina responded, "I got enough to pay for my school, so I don't have to work. Once I get that CNA certificate, that'll mean more money for me and my kids."

Chip looked up at me and said, "Then why wait?"

I thought about what Chip said. He had a point, but there was still more money to be made and I wanted it. "Three more months and that'll be it. I promise," I said.

SWIPE

Mia spoke out. "I'm down for that."

Trina said, "Me too."

We all looked at Chip. "Although I don't agree with it, for you, China, I'll continue my part."

"Settled. The countdown is on. So ladies turn it up." I looked at Chip. "Let's make that money. Drink up."

I finished off the rest of the champagne in the glass.

Chip cleared his throat. He pointed at his watch.

Trina stood up. "Y'all ain't the only ones who have something to do. My man's coming over, and I promised him a home cooked meal, so we're out of here."

"Hold up. Your man? I didn't even know you were seeing anyone," I said.

"Don't have time to tell you about him now. I'll tell you later. Come on, Mia," Trina said as she rushed out the front door.

Chip laughed at me. "You did practically kick them out."

"I didn't say a thing."

"Well, your facial expression said it all. Forget Trina right now. The rest of the night is ours. Go get dressed so we can get out of here."

Two hours later, we were finishing up our dinner at one of the local casinos.

"Baby, I'm feeling lucky. Let's go play poker," Chip said.

"I can be your wing man," I said.

"What you know about poker?" Chip asked.

"More than you think. Watch and learn, amateur," I teased.

KAYENNE

Chip and I took turns watching each other play at the regular poker tables. He was a skilled player and so was I.

I looped my arm in Chip's arm and whispered, "Now that we've played with these amateurs, let's amp it up. Let's take it to the high rollers table."

"Both of us don't need to be at the table," Chip responded.

"I'll sit it out. I'll let you do your thing. I'll be there for support . . . and distraction."

Chip smiled. He knew with me wearing the low-cut, black sequined dress, that some of the men would be trying to steal a glance.

We walked to the door. The attendant said, "Each chip is a thousand in this room."

I walked up in front of Chip. "Did we ask you that? We want in."

"Ma'am, I'm just saying," the attendant said.

I interrupted him. "First of all, I'm too young to be a ma'am, and secondly, if we couldn't afford to play, we wouldn't be here, so please let us in the room."

The attendant looked up behind Chip. Two security guards walked up behind us.

One of the guards asked the attendant, "Is there a problem?"

The attendant looked down at me. I had a scowl on my face. "The problem is me and my man have money to play poker and this joker won't let us in."

"Is that true?" the security guard asked.

"I didn't know. It's my job to make sure everyone knows what the minimum is before they gain access."

SWIPE

"We're sorry for your inconvenience. Now let the lady and gentleman inside," the security guard directed the attendant.

The attendant mumbled something under his breath. I smiled and then licked my tongue out at him as he allowed Chip and me access.

Chip whispered, "You already causing a scene with your bad self."

"You like it when I'm bad."

I walked out in front of him so he could see me twist. I stopped, looked back at him, and saw him smile.

One of the lady attendants walked up to me. "Can I help you?"

I responded, "Yes, my man there would like to sit in on the next round."

"Have a seat over there. This game is ending. Next one will be starting in about fifteen minutes."

Chip and I practically danced out of the casino. We walked out twenty-five thousand dollars richer. Chip agreed to share half of the proceeds with me. I stopped and kissed him.

"So this is why you decided to divorce me?" I heard Gerry's voice from behind me.

I stopped kissing Chip and turned to see Gerry and some blonde floozy holding on to his arm.

"Don't even try that shit with me," I responded. "You were the one who cheated, remember?"

"Dear, if you're going to start dating again, raise your standards. My shoes cost more than his whole outfit," Gerry said.

I stood directly in front of Chip, and I could sense him getting upset by his heavy breathing. "Baby, I got this," I said to Chip, before turning to look at Gerry. "Chip has more style in his pinky finger than you have in your entire body."

"*Chip*. Well, *Chip*, how does it feel to have my leftovers?"

I couldn't control Chip then. He grabbed Gerry around the collar. His date yelled out, "No, don't hurt him!"

Chip shouted, "I'm going to teach you how to show some respect. Now apologize to China."

Gerry's voice shook when he talked. "Get your hands off me, or I'll have you arrested!"

I grabbed Chip's raised hand before he could punch Gerry. "Baby, he's not worth it."

Chip let Gerry go.

Gerry fell back on his date. He held his neck from where Chip had him in a tight grip. Fear filled his eyes. Gerry was used to giving out the orders, not taking them.

"If I ever hear of you disrespecting China again, not even she will be able to save you from my wrath." Chip grabbed my hand and pulled me along with him.

SWIPE

CHAPTER TWENTY-EIGHT
Trina

The first time Dale and I slept together was the only time we used a condom. He'd been going raw dog in me ever since, and I'm not going to lie, it felt good. It felt so good that I think I was becoming addicted to the dick. When neither one of us was working, we were spending time together. Between the kids and his altering shift, we got it in whenever we could. That sort of kept things exciting between us, because we never knew when we would be able to do so without an interruption.

Today was no different. He was supposed to be making his rounds, but instead he took a detour and was now in my bathroom showering so he could finish his shift. I hoped one of my nosy neighbors didn't report him.

I sat on the bed and watched him get dressed. He smiled at me.

"Have you thought about what I said?" he asked.

"I would love to move in with you, but what happens when you get tired of me? Me and my kids will be out on the streets."

"I can never get tired of you. These last six weeks of being with you has changed my life. I love you. I love the kids."

"I love you too, but that's not enough for me to up and move in with you," I said.

"I understand." He sat on the edge of the bed and laced up his black boots.

"Are you mad at me?"

He turned and looked at me. "No, I'm not mad. I respect what you had to say. If you were my sister, I wouldn't expect you to up and move in with a guy you're not married to either."

"So you do get it."

"Yes, but I'm not going to stop trying to convince you." He turned and bounced on me and kissed me.

"You better stop before you get your uniform wrinkled." I walked Dale to the door and gave him another kiss. "Shreveport's finest, don't give out too many tickets," I said.

"I'll try not to. Tell the crazy drivers to stay off the street." He kissed me one more time before leaving.

I felt like the women I read about in them Urban novels. I can't pinpoint the moment I fell in love with Dale, but I was in love. He was my Black Knight. My King. The light of my world. My kids adored him and I loved him.

Mia kept getting on me about ending it, but I was too caught up to end it. This relationship was the best relationship I ever had, and I wasn't going to mess it up.

Around one in the afternoon, I picked up the kids from school because they had doctor's appointments. I daydreamed about life with Dale as I waited for us to be called to the back. All the kids got a clean bill of health.

SWIPE

Hours later, we were back at home. They were in their room and I was laid back on the couch thinking about Dale. I picked up my phone and sent Dale a text to let him know I changed my mind. I was going to take a chance and move in with him.

I turned on the ten o'clock news. My mouth flew open when I heard the reporter say, "Officer Dale Warner has been shot. We have no word on his condition."

I couldn't breathe. I grabbed my phone and dialed his number. Instead of his voice mail answering, some woman's voice was on the other end.

"Who is this?" I yelled.

"Are you calling about Dale?" the woman responded.

"Yes, but who is this?" My heart felt like it was about to jump out of my chest. *Please tell me this is not a wife. Not again.*

"This is his mother."

I sighed with relief. "I'm Trina. Dale's girlfriend."

"Yes, I've heard about you. Dale's in surgery, baby."

I didn't want to ask but I needed to know. "Is he going to live?" I blurted out before I lost the nerves to ask.

"I don't know. The doctor's haven't told me anything." She started crying.

"As soon as I get someone to watch my kids, I'll be there."

She told me what hospital she was at. I called some of my relatives, but no one would answer their phones. I checked in on the kids to see if they were still sleeping and they were. I didn't like to leave them

KAYENNE

for long periods of time, but I would just go to the hospital, check on Dale and return. They would be all right, I told myself as I found a jacket to put on.

After I made sure the house was secure, I rushed toward the hospital. It seemed like each traffic light caught me and was long. When I walked into the emergency room, I knew immediately which woman was Dale's mom because she was surrounded and being comforted by several police officers.

I stood back and watched as the officers paced the floor. Some were on their phones and others were talking to each other. Dale's mom must have sensed someone was watching. She looked up into my eyes. Our eyes locked. She got up from where she sat and walked up to me. Without saying another word, we hugged.

"Mrs. Warner," a young doctor came out into the emergency room and called out.

She turned around. "I'm right here."

The entire emergency room got quiet. The doctor walked up to her.

"Your son has lost a lot of blood. These next twenty-four to forty-eight hours are critical. He's in ICU. You and your daughter can come back to see him, but you can only stay a few minutes."

I opened my mouth to say I wasn't her daughter, but she grabbed my hand. I followed her and the doctor toward the ICU. The police officers moved aside so we could have a clear path. As soon as we went through the doors, I could hear the chatter starting back up from behind us.

The doctor said, "I wanted you to see him because bringing loved ones around helps the patient.

He hasn't opened his eyes yet, but he can probably hear you, so talk to him as if he was looking at you."

He opened the door to the room and my heart dropped seeing Dale hooked up to all of those monitors. His mom ran up to the bed. "My baby. Mama loves you," she repeated over and over. I watched her rub his face and kiss his forehead. "Baby, I got somebody here to see you." She motioned with her hand for me to come closer.

I did as she directed. I was scared to touch him because I didn't want any of the tubes to move causing more damage.

"Hey, baby. It's me." I held his hand. "I don't know if you got my message . . . before . . . well, I wanted you to know that the answer is yes. Yes to your question. I love you, so you got to get better so we can start the life we wanted."

The doctor returned to the room. "I'm afraid time's up."

"Mama loves you," his mom said before walking out.

I remained behind for a few seconds. "I love you, Dale. The kids love you too."

I didn't exhale until I left the room, and his mom and I fell into each other's arms sobbing.

KAYENNE

CHAPTER TWENTY-EIGHT
Mia

"Mia, isn't that your friend on the news?" one of my co-workers asked me in the break room at work as soon as my shift started. It was only eight something in the morning. We were there early to do inventory.

I looked up at the television. The report was about the shooting of an officer. There were scenes from the emergency room in the hospital. And there, seated right next to some woman I didn't know was my best friend Trina.

I pulled out my phone and dialed Trina's number.

"Hello." She sounded sleepy.

"Trina, what's going on?"

"Dale's been shot."

"I saw you on the news."

"For real? I was hoping I wasn't going to be on there."

"I'm at work, but I'm about to clock out. Where are you?"

"I'm at home now. I'm going to take a shower and then go back up there. I came back to get the kids ready for school."

"Did you leave the kids by themselves? Never mind. Don't answer that. Don't go nowhere until I get there."

SWIPE

I hung up with her and faced my co-worker. "I hope y'all got enough people to cover my shift because I'm gone for today."

"You just got here," my co-worker said.

"I got a family emergency. I got to go."

I located my supervisor and told her the situation. She let me off without any issues. I broke several traffic laws getting over to Trina's. She was coming out of her house when I pulled up.

"Trina, didn't I tell you to wait on me? Hop your ass in the car." I put my head out my window.

I sort of felt bad for yelling at her when I saw how pitiful she looked when she got in the car.

"He's at University Health. I promised his mama I would come back. Besides, I need to be there when he wakes up."

"You really love that man, don't you?"

"Yes, that's what I've been trying to tell you. What we got is special. I can't lose him. I just can't." She started crying.

"Look in the glove compartment. There's some tissue in there," I said.

Like the dutiful friend that I am, I drove her to the hospital and waited with her in the emergency room. I felt uncomfortable being around all of the police officers that came in and out. I tried to stay out of the way and sit in a corner, but some of the men would find themselves near me and attempted to drum up a conversation. I would smile and then hold my hand up flashing my one carat diamond wedding ring. That said more than words could. They would then make an excuse to keep it moving.

KAYENNE

"Mrs. Warner," one of the doctors came out and said.

The room got quiet. Dale's mom walked near him. "Doctor, please tell me you have good news about my son."

Trina stood near her.

The doctor responded, "He's been upgraded to stable. Mrs. Warner, he would like to see you and Trina."

Trina blurted out, "He's awake."

"Praise the Lord!" Mrs. Warner shouted.

"Yes, he's awake. But let me warn you, he's still not fully coherent, but you both can see him. Only for a short time," the doctor said.

Trina left with Mrs. Warner. I didn't feel too comfortable being around all of these police officers, so I sent Trina a short text mentioning I was going to get something to eat and eased out to my car.

I couldn't locate my phone charger. I looked under the seat and finally located it. My cell phone rang. China's number displayed across the screen.

"I saw Trina on the news surrounded by a whole bunch of cops, what the fuck is going on?" she yelled from the other end of the phone.

"Hold on," I said. I located my Bluetooth and put it on my ear. I started up the car and headed to get Trina and me a burger. "It's complicated."

"Mia, I don't have time for no games."

China could get on my nerves sometimes with her acting like she was in control of us. "Trina's boyfriend was the officer that got shot, so that's why you saw her on TV."

SWIPE

"Boyfriend? Why am I just now hearing this? Did you know she was seeing a cop?" she blurted out question after question.

"Yes, I knew. I thought she had stopped, but she hadn't."

"I don't know what was going through her mind with all we got going on that she would be dating a cop."

"Calm down, China. If you want to talk about that, you should probably call me on my other number."

"How can I be calm when Trina's sleeping with the enemy?"

"Trina would never do anything to jeopardize what we got going on," I assured her, although I wasn't too sure of things anymore myself.

"I'm coming up there. I need to see what's going on myself."

"You might not want to do that. The hospital waiting area is like police central. Besides, you might not want to be seen with us low lives."

"Mia, now is not the time with you and your attitude. Tell Trina to call me ASAP."

"I will when I get back to the hospital. I just left to get us something to eat."

"I'll send Chip over there to talk to her," China mumbled.

Regardless, if neither one of them actually admitted something was going on between the two of them, I knew it was. He and China were always together. He was too familiar with the place for him not to be living there.

KAYENNE

"Mia, are you there?" I heard China say, after tuning her out for a minute.

"Yeah. I'm driving."

"Don't forget. She needs to call me today, not tomorrow. I got to go." China hung up the phone.

Between China and Trina's drama, I was getting a headache. Didn't they know I had enough problems of my own to deal with—like a maniac husband still trying to control things from inside the prison walls.

CHAPTER TWENTY-NINE
China

I couldn't get any rest after getting off the phone with Mia. I flipped the television station from news channel to news channel. There Trina was on each and every one of them as they discussed the officer's shooting.

They still hadn't caught the suspect guilty of firing the bullets.

Mia was right. I definitely didn't need to be seen there. The cameraman might zoom in on me, and the last thing I needed was to be featured on the news. Gerry would have definitely been reaching out to me then.

Chip grabbed my hand and the remote. "You need to get a grip. Besides, I'm tired of you changing the channel." He put it on one local station and placed the remote on the other side of him.

"I can reach the remote if I want to," I shouted.

"But you will have to come through me to get it, and you're off remote duty as of right now."

"Oh yeah?" I said.

"Yes!"

He and I had a playful banter for a few minutes with me ending up on top of him. I looked down and got drawn into his dreamy eyes. Our lips touched and we kissed.

"You know exactly how to calm me down," I said as I moved and sat up.

He sat up next to me. "We've been dating long enough for me to figure you out."

"I think Mia is jealous of our relationship," I said.

"You want to spoil a perfectly good conversation by bringing up Mia."

"I'm just saying. I can tell from the way she acts."

"You know you women. If she is, that's her personal problem. That has nothing to do with you or me." Chip pulled me into his arms. I ended up laying my head upon his chest.

"I was hoping Mia and I could get back to the way things used to be with us, but I don't know if that's even possible." I frowned.

"Sometimes friends grow apart. Don't beat yourself up about it."

"I do miss our talks. She was like a sister to me."

"You've mentioned that before. You also mentioned that Trina was like a sister to you, so don't you think you should be getting dressed and going to be with your friend while she's going through this?" Chip asked.

I shifted my body and then looked up into his eyes. "I will. When she's no longer at the hospital. I don't want to be around a whole bunch of cops. I would get the hives."

"Just remember, to have a friend you need to be a friend."

I playfully hit him on the chest. "Okay, ghetto professor. You're always trying to be a philosopher."

SWIPE

Three days later, I took Chip's advice. I went to Trina's house and knocked on the door for what seemed like ten minutes before she finally came to it.

"What took you so long to open the door?" I asked as soon as she appeared in the open door.

"I was sleep," she responded, wearing a wrinkled top and pants.

"I've been calling you." I walked past her and took a seat on the couch.

She rubbed her eyes. "I'd planned on calling you back, but between the kids and going to the hospital, I just haven't had the time."

"So why am I the last to know you're dating a cop?"

We both sat on her couch.

"I didn't think I had to tell you what was going on in my personal life. You don't share nothing with me. When we talk, it's always about business. Every now and then you'll ask me about the kids or give me something to give the kids."

I didn't sound like too much of a friend by the way she talked. I guess I needed to do a reevaluation of myself. "We're still girls. At least I thought we were."

"When it's convenient for you," she responded.

"You're sounding like Mia now."

"No, I'm sounding like myself. When was the last time we got together to just hang out?"

I looked up in the air and thought about it. "I can't remember."

"Neither can I. But anyway, right now I don't have time to hang out. As soon as I get dressed I'm going back up to the hospital."

KAYENNE

"What about the kids?" I asked.

"They're going over to their play aunt's house," Trina responded.

"I can get them if you need me to," I suggested.

"No, that's okay. I don't want to inconvenience you."

"I'm serious."

"Maybe another time. I've already instructed the bus driver to drop the kids off at her house."

"Anything else you need me to do while I'm here?" I asked.

"You can go to the hospital with me," she said.

She left and went to finish getting dressed. I contemplated on what to do next. Should I or shouldn't I go were the two questions I pondered back and forth in my mind.

It didn't take long for Trina to come back fully dressed in some tight jeans and a T-shirt.

"Girl, those sure are tight," I commented.

"Naw, these are the loose fit. You should see the tight ones," she responded.

"You definitely got a badonk-a-donk," I teased.

"Are you ready?" she asked.

"Trina, under the circumstances, I don't think me going to the hospital would be a good idea. We don't need anyone tying us together."

"Whatever. I got to go, so you got to go," she responded with an attitude.

She walked to the door dangling her keys.

I stood up and followed her out the door. "How long do you plan on being up there?" I asked.

"I'll probably spend the night."

"What about work?" I asked.

SWIPE

"I told them I needed time off until further notice."

"But . . ."

Trina held up her hand. "It sounds to me like you're only concerned about *the business*."

"That's not true," I attempted to assure her. "I care about you, and I care about your man, even though I don't know him."

"Well, you have a funny way of showing it." Trina got in her car without saying another word.

I went to my black late model BMW that was parked on the street. She pulled out of the driveway and left me sitting there contemplating on when I became such a bad friend.

KAYENNE

CHAPTER THIRTY
Trina

The next six weeks went by in a blur for me. I juggled time with the kids and going to the rehabilitation hospital where Dale had to re-learn how to walk. He'd fully gained his senses and mobility since the shooting. I still worked but I cut my hours down.

China didn't seem too thrilled that I barely turned in five cards a week, but fuck her. Seeing about my family and man were more important right now. Besides, I still got my half whether I turned in five or fifty.

Mia tried to talk me out of moving in with Dale, but I wouldn't listen to her either. Dale getting shot sealed the deal for us. Neither one of us wanted to waste any more time. His friends from the police force came by one day and moved all of my stuff for me.

Mia protested about that too, but it wasn't like she was helping me move, so she didn't have a say so on that either.

Dale was at home, and between his mother and me, we made sure he was comfortable. A rehabilitation nurse was assigned to come out to the house every other day on the days he didn't have to go to the hospital.

Tonight, Dale and I lay in bed, while the kids were in the living room watching TV.

Dale squeezed his arm around me. "I'm so lucky to have you in my life. Some of my friends are jealous."

"Why is that?" I asked.

"Because they wish they had what we have."

I looked into his eyes. "And what do we have?"

"This." He shifted his body until we were face to face.

He cupped my face with his hand and kissed me on my top lip and then my bottom lip. Once our lips touched, he eased his tongue inside my mouth and our tongues tangled back and forth in each other's mouth.

We inhaled and exhaled and it felt as if we'd become one.

Yasmin burst in the room yelling, "Mama, X, hit me!"

We stopped kissing. I turned toward Yasmin. "Yas, how many times have I told you, you need to knock when you see a door closed?"

"I did knock," Yasmin responded, looking innocent.

"Dale, baby, I'll be right back. Let me go check on these kids."

I followed Yasmin into the living room and caught Xavier and Zahara wrestling on the floor. I grabbed Zahara and pulled her off Xavier. "Stop it and stop it now. Because y'all want to fight, you can each go to your rooms."

KAYENNE

Xavier licked out his tongue at Zahara. "I'm glad I got my own room now so I don't have to watch you suck your thumb."

"I don't suck my thumb," Zahara responded. "You big cry baby."

Xavier ran toward her. I blocked him. "X, go to your room. Now!"

Zahara said, "Na na—"

"Za, you say one more thing and you're gonna get the ass whooping you've been wanting all week. Why are you doing all of this fighting?"

"Because X keeps messing with us!" Yasmin said.

"Y'all kids need to learn how to get along. Dale's been nice enough to let us come stay with him, so we need to respect his house. Understood?"

Yasmin and Zahara looked at each other. Neither said anything.

"Oh. Since both of y'all want to pretend like y'all can't talk. Take your asses to your room. No TV."

"But, Mama!" Yasmin said.

"No, buts. Take your asses to bed and maybe tomorrow you'll wake up with a better attitude."

Yasmin and Zahara pouted and slung their arms when they walked toward their room.

I straightened up the living room by placing the pillows back on the couch. Dale's place was larger than mine. He lived in a three-bedroom house with a nice backyard located in the Southern Hills neighborhood. The only thing I didn't like was Lucky, his big rottweiler who Dale swore was still a puppy. Lucky barked every time I went to the back door. I don't think Lucky liked me, although Dale disagreed.

SWIPE

The kids loved the dog and the dog seemed to love them. I'd never been a dog lover, so maybe that's why the dog didn't like me. He could sense it.

"Can you bring me some water?" Dale yelled out from his bedroom.

Dale was like the fourth child. I didn't know who to say was more demanding, him or the triplets.

I returned to the bedroom. "Dale, what are you doing?"

Dale looked up at me and held up a credit card? "Who is Tracy Baker?"

Aw shit. I had to think of something and think of something quick. I handed him the water and took the card from his hand. "That's a friend from work. I was low on cash and she let me use her card to get gas. I guess I forgot to give it back to her. I'm going to text her now and let her know I got it." I dropped the card in my purse and got out my cell phone. Instead of texting Tracy, I sent a text to Mia, who responded right away. I looked up at Dale. "She said thanks because she was just about to call to cancel it because she couldn't find it."

"Good thing I did."

I hope he hadn't been snooping in my purse. If so, this move might not have been a good one after all. "Where did you find it?" I asked as I slipped in beside him on the bed.

"It was on the floor. I saw it when I tried to get the remote."

"It must have fallen out of my clothes when I took them off," I lied.

"Trina, if you ever need some money, let me know. You don't have to go begging from someone else."

"I wasn't begging. Me and Lisa help each other out all of the time."

"Who is Lisa?" Dale asked.

"I mean Tracy. Me and Tracy do that for each other all of the time."

"I'm just saying. I'm your man and I take care of what's mine."

"But you haven't been working. You told me you won't get but a portion of your salary until the doctor releases you to go back to work. I don't want to burden you."

"Baby, there's something I should have told you, but haven't. When I tell you, you have to promise that you won't share it with anybody."

"I won't," I said.

"I mean it, Trina. Not even with your friend Mia."

This must be serious. "I promise. I won't share it with anyone."

His phone rang and interrupted us. "Baby, I got to take this call. Can you make me a sandwich?"

"Sure."

I left the room, but my curiosity was peaked. He needed to hurry and get off the phone, so we could finish our conversation.

CHAPTER THIRTY-ONE
Mia

My buddy, the security guard, met me outside of the break room.

"You don't be around much. They cut your hours?" he asked as he blocked the entranceway.

"Yes. You know how they do around here."

"I need to talk to you for a minute. Can you come with me to the control room?"

I glanced at the wall clock. "I don't have but a fifteen minute break."

"Fifteen. I don't need but ten," he said with a huge grin on his face.

I really didn't have time to fool with this clown, but I entertained him and followed him to the control room.

As soon as the door was closed, Sam was all up on me. I used my hand to push him away. "Wait a minute. You know I'm a married woman."

"I ain't never seen a husband. You one of those who like to fake like they got a husband by putting on a fake ring."

I held my hand out and showed him my real one carat diamond ring. "Ain't nothing fake about this."

"Well, your husband's not here." He attempted to kiss me.

I blocked him with my hand. "Sam, you need to back up off me."

Big Belly started unbuckling his pants. He laughed. "I know what you've been doing. I've been watching you."

"So what? That's what you get paid to do . . . watch people." I crossed my arms.

By now he'd unzipped his pants. "I need my dick sucked."

"Then you better find somebody to do it."

"I have. You."

"You've lost your mind if you think I'm going to suck your shriveled up limp dick," I blurted.

Where was his supervisor when I needed him? He needed to burst in and catch him so his ass could get fired.

"I saw you swiping those people's cards. I got it on tape too, so you can go to jail. But if you suck my dick, your little secret will remain safe with me," he assured me.

Sam eased up closer to me. I could smell his hot, tart breath. I grabbed him by the balls and squeezed. He screeched out in pain. "I told you, I'm not sucking nothing!"

"Oh, you will. I'll give you twenty-four hours to change your mind. After that, if you don't start slobbing on this knob . . ." He grabbed his dick so I could see it. "I'm turning in the video."

"Fuck you, Sam!" I burst out the door and rushed past the elderly security guard, who was now walking toward the control room.

SWIPE

I went back to the employees' lockers and pulled out my cell phone. I sent Chip a quick text message.

The rest of my shift was spent looking up toward the camera. When no customers were in sight, I threw up my middle finger toward the camera just in case Sam was looking.

The phone near the register rang.

"Women's clothing, how may I help you?" I said when I answered.

"Have you changed your mind yet?" Sam asked.

"Are these phones taped or monitored?" I asked.

"No. We can tell which numbers call what, but not the conversation."

"So you're in the control room?"

"I was. I'm in hardware. I didn't want my supervisor to know I was calling."

"Maybe we can work something out. Meet me at the hotel on Lakeshore. Room 122 when you get off."

"Ooh wee. I'm getting hard just thinking about the things I'm going to do with you."

I grabbed my stomach. I felt queasy. "Come as soon as you get off."

"You don't have to tell me twice."

Our call ended. The rest of the time at work went by slow. Sam looked like a broke down version of Biggie Small, and just the thought of him touching me made me want to puke.

Four hours later, I was in the hotel room and Sam was knocking on the door. The hotel was more like a motel. It wasn't in the best of neighborhoods, and the people who frequented this motel weren't always up to any good. It was the perfect spot to meet Sam.

KAYENNE

I opened the door and he walked in carrying a brown paperback and two plastic cups. "I stopped at the liquor store and got us some dranks."

"Great minds think alike. I'd already stopped and got something."

"For real? I'll save my stuff for later." He put the bag on the table near the television.

He didn't waste any time taking off his clothes. Seeing him completely naked was even more disgusting than imagining him naked.

Sam hopped in the bed with his dick shooting straight up in the air. It had the width of a smoke sausage, but couldn't have been any more than four inches in length. He patted the bed beside him. "Come on, girl. Whatcha waiting for?"

I turned my back to him and poured him a drink. I handed it to him. "Drink up and then we can get straight to business."

"That's what I'm talking about." He took the drink from me and turned it up, drinking every drop.

"You ready for me?" I said as I did a seductive dance.

"Come to daddy," he said right before his body started shivering.

His eyes rolled from side to side. Foam seeped out of the corners of his mouth. The glass he held fell to the bed. I grabbed the glass and placed it back in the bag that it was in. Then I removed my small handbag and placed it and the spiked liquor in my purse.

He should have known that something was up because I was wearing gloves. Satisfied that Sam would no longer be a threat, I eased out of the hotel room unnoticed by anyone and slipped through a side gate that led to a side street where my car was parked.

When I got on the main road, I called Chip. "It's handled."

Sam wouldn't be threatening to expose me or anyone else for that matter ever again.

KAYENNE

CHAPTER THIRTY-TWO
China

I threw a pillow at Chip. "Damn, why didn't you tell me? I can't believe y'all killed somebody," I said. "Nobody was supposed to die behind this."

Chip hit his chest. "I'm the enforcer, right? That's what I do. Someone in my circle has a problem and I handle it."

"But killing an innocent man. It could have been handled a different way."

"Mia said he was going to show some video footage to the police. I had no choice."

"There are always choices."

"Fuck, China. What would you have done?"

"I don't know, but I wouldn't have killed him."

"Too late now. It's a done deal."

"I know." I plopped down on the bed with my back toward Chip. "This was supposed to be simple. Nobody was supposed to die. Nobody," I said over and over.

Chip grabbed me from behind and wrapped his arms around me and rocked me back and forth.

"It couldn't be avoided."

"I know but still . . . I didn't expect this."

The doorbell rang. "That's Mia," Chip said.

SWIPE

"At this time of night? What is she doing here?"

Chip walked down the stairs with me not too far behind him. He looked through the peephole and opened up the door.

Mia walked in looking high.

"Have you been drinking?" I asked.

"Yes, a little bit. I drunk something and was riding around and ended up here."

"Why didn't you go home?" I asked.

"Look. After the kind of day I had, I don't have time for your fifty and one questions," she snapped.

Chip asked, "Do you have the stuff?"

Mia pulled out a bag and a glass and handed it to Chip. "This is it."

"You ladies talk. I'm going to dispose of this."

"Not in my trash can," I blurted.

Chip kissed me on the cheek. "I got this. Trust me."

I threw my hand in the air. "Come on, Mia. I'm going to make you some coffee."

"I don't want any coffee. I need a drink. I just killed a man. I've never done anything like this before."

"Why didn't you call me? We could have thought of something else," I said as we walked to the kitchen.

"I panicked and Chip's the only one besides Tony that I know could handle a situation like this. That bastard wanted me to suck his little dick."

"Was it little?" I asked.

By now we're in the kitchen. I retrieved a box of gourmet coffee out of the pantry.

"It was this little. Look at me," Mia said.

KAYENNE

I turned to look at her and Mia used her hands to illustrate the size. "Girl, you could have sucked that."

"His breath smelled like hot garbage, so you could imagine how his dick would smell."

"You do have a point there."

We both laughed.

Chip walked in. "I'm glad you ladies have found something to laugh about."

"No thanks to you," I said.

Chip ignored me and addressed Mia. "You made sure no one saw you, right?"

"Of course. And even if I left any hair strands, it will come back in a lab test as Yaki 1B 30."

Chip laughed. "Mia, you're crazy. Ladies, I'll leave you two alone." Chip kissed me lightly on the lips and walked out.

"Are you happy?" Mia asked.

"Some days." I located two big coffee mugs.

"Does Chip make you happy?"

"Yes. Very much so."

"That's good. I don't know what happiness is anymore," Mia confessed.

"Have you considered divorcing Tony?" I asked.

The buzzer went off on the coffee to alert me that it was ready. I poured us two cups as we continued to talk.

"I thought about it, but then that would be wrong to dump a man when he's locked up."

"No, it wouldn't," I said. "If the situation was reversed, do you think Tony would wait for you?"

She tilted her head as if in deep thought. "Probably not."

"Probably not. Come on. Be for real," I said, handing her the sugar container.

"Hell naw. He would have some other chick up in the same bed we shared." She poured some sugar in her coffee.

"Then if you're unhappy. It's time to make yourself happy. Take back control of your life."

For once Mia and I had a civil conversation without either one of us getting an attitude.

Mia looked at me and said, "You're right. It's time for Mia to be happy. Tony can kiss my ass!"

KAYENNE

CHAPTER THIRTY-THREE
Trina

How long are you gonna be? I thought before I fell asleep waiting on Dale to get off the phone. He received back to back phone calls from family and friends checking up on his health. I didn't want to complain to him about it, so I just turned over and read a romance novel until I dozed off.

I dreamed an earthquake had hit and the whole house was shaking. I reached out for Dale but he wasn't near. "Dale!" I screamed out. I woke up and felt Dale shaking me.

"Trina, are you all right?" he asked.

"I was having a nightmare." I sat up in the bed, grabbing my pounding head. "You got any aspirin? My head is killing me."

"Yes. In the top cabinet."

I went to the bathroom and found the pills. I took one and put water in my hands and drank it to wash the pills down.

Dale was walking through the door before I could exit. I smiled.

"Why you looking at me like that?" he asked.

"Look at you. You're walking. Not limping."

He grabbed me by my waist. "And it's all because of you."

"No. It's because of God. Your mama's been talking to me about church and thangs."

"You're right. God spared my life. It's some changes I need to make. One of them concerns you."

I frowned. "We just got here. You want us to move already."

He squeezed me tighter. "No, baby. It's all good. One of my friends is going to come pick me up and take me somewhere, and when I get back I promise we're going to finish the conversation I started last night."

"I hope so. I tried to stay up but I was tired."

"You are off today, aren't you?" he asked.

"No. I go in for a few hours."

"I want you to think about going to school full time. I can handle the bills."

"Really? If I go full time I can have my CNA license in less than a year."

"Then do it. Put in your notice today."

"Don't you want to think about it first?"

"Nothing to think about. We're going to be together, so no need for you to be working and trying to take care of the kids and go to school. Let me ease your load, baby." Dale kissed me. He had me under his spell. "So what are you going to do?"

"I'm quitting."

I called Mia on the way to work. "Dale wants me to quit. Says he has enough to take care of us. I can go to school full time."

"You haven't known him long enough," Mia said.

KAYENNE

"We're living together, so the amount of time doesn't matter now," I responded.

"Trina, I think if you quit, you'll be making a big mistake."

"Oh, so you and China the only two that can have men taking care of you. He's the first guy I've been with that said, 'baby, you ain't got to work.'"

"It's not like that. If I had to do it over, when Tony was giving me all of that money, I would have taken my ass to school. But instead I spent it all and don't have shit to show for it now."

"You can do like I'm about to do. With your money you got now, take some classes."

"Only thing I'm good at is hustling and there's no degree for that," Mia responded.

"You like to spend . . . I mean, manage folks money, so go get you a business degree or something."

"You got jokes. But don't be trying to change the subject."

"I've made up my mind. I'm quitting. The only reason I'm going in to work today is so I can get some more numbers."

"Do what you want? Can't say I didn't try to warn you."

An hour later, I eased my car into the parking lot. The place was busy. I still had another hour before the lunch hour crowd. I got ready for my shift. I would have to wait until after one to whip out the credit card device.

We must have been running a special on burgers because we had back to back customers. When I went on break I decided to go ahead and use the machine.

SWIPE

This was my last day, and I needed to get all of the cards I could scan since I wouldn't be doing this anymore.

As I took orders in the drive-thru I heard, "We need to talk," China said from her car.

She startled me because I wasn't expecting to see her.

"That'll be seven twenty-two, ma'am. Cash or credit?"

China tilted her head and looked up in my direction. "Free."

I practically threw her the bag.

"Call me as soon as you go on break," China stated before she pulled off.

I took a short break an hour later and called her.

"Mia told me you were quitting." China didn't waste any time getting straight to the point.

"I am. Dale's going to foot the bills at the house so I can go to school full time."

"I thought we agreed to do this three more months."

"It's been two months. Quitting one month early is not going to hurt anything."

"It messes up our operation. You need to reconsider what you're about to do."

I was sick and tired of China and Mia thinking they could walk over me and dictate what went on in my life. "I've made up my mind."

I hung up the phone while China was still talking.

"Trina, we getting super busy again. We need you up front," the supervisor said.

KAYENNE

I went back to my station, and my coworker Lisa said, "I tried using the scanner, but it wouldn't work right. Have you been able to get it to work?"

Oh no! I couldn't believe I left the scanner near the register. I bit my bottom lip. Trying to think of something to say. "Did you tell anybody else about it?"

"Naw. I got it to work when I ran it like we normally do. That's why I don't like working drive-thru. It's always something."

"Girl, don't worry about it. I'll have someone look at it."

"I'm glad you're back so I can get back to my station."

As soon as she left, I removed the device that was about the size of a cell phone and placed it in my pocket.

"Trina, when your shift ends I want to see you," Michael, the new evening supervisor said.

"Okay. I need to talk to you too."

I was glad I'd used the machine earlier because I couldn't risk pulling it out any more. China's the reason I didn't get more numbers.

Michael was seated behind the desk when I entered the office area.

He looked up at me. "Have a seat." I did as instructed. He went on to say. "I was informed of a problem with the cash register. You've been working it most of the day. Have you had any problems? I need to know so I can call it in."

I crossed my legs. "I don't know about any problems. It worked fine for me."

"Lisa said she tried to scan some of the customer credit cards and the transactions didn't go through."

I wasn't too surprised that Lisa lied to me. "Like I said, I didn't have any problems. You can check my register."

"Believe me, I will later."

"She mentioned she was having problems, but I didn't have time to show her how to use the register. If she knew how to use the other register, I figured she wouldn't have a problem using the one in drive-thru." I could feel the sweat forming on my forehead. I was too nervous to even wipe it from my head.

"Maybe it's Lisa then. We might have to put her in another position." Michael stared at me. He was making me nervous. Real nervous. I wished he wouldn't look me in the eyes.

I blinked several times, uncrossed my legs, and leaned a little forward. "Between you and me, Lisa is a little slow. I didn't want to say anything before 'cause I didn't want her to lose her job or nothing."

"Thanks for your input. We're going to see how she does as one of the cooks."

I exhaled as soon as I left out of the office. I thought I'd been busted. I was so busy trying to make sure I hadn't been that I forgot to quit.

KAYENNE

CHAPTER THIRTY-FOUR
Mia

Trina sat on my couch and rehashed the story of what happened at work. "I thought I was busted for sure," she said.

I smoked on a blunt and handed it to her. "So what you gonna do?"

"I'm calling in sick every day. Let them fire me. I might even be able to get some unemployment."

"You might as well. You quit. You won't get nothing from unemployment."

Trina looked at the time. "I need to go. I have to talk to Dale before the kids get out of school."

"You realize that you barely have a conversation without mentioning his name."

"Mia, you don't understand. Dale's the best man I ever had. He treats me and the kids well. He's not like some of these other dudes that just want to smash it. He actually cares about me."

I pretended to play a violin. "Love's no fairytale. Enjoy these moments as long as you can."

"With Dale I ain't got to worry about if the law's going to arrest him, he is the law."

SWIPE

"Yes. He's the law sleeping with a criminal. If he only knew who he had sleeping in his bed."

Trina threw up her middle finger. "He knew I was ratchet when he met me, but it didn't matter. I think he likes the fact that I gets mine."

"Naw, he likes that fat ass of yours. Keep it one hundred."

Trina laughed. "The ass gets them every time."

"You know it." We high-fived each other.

Trina left and went home to her man while I was left sitting on the couch contemplating what I was going to do to fill the void in my life.

I decided to take another unscheduled trip to visit my friend China. We'd made up, so why not?

China didn't seem too happy to see me when I showed up unannounced, but I didn't care. I made myself at home. I invited myself to dinner and ate until I couldn't eat any more. She and Chip looked at me like I'd lost my mind.

I hadn't. I was just lonely.

We were now seated in the living room. Each one of us had our drink of choice. I was sipping on a glass of merlot. "This some of that good stuff," I said as I poured another glass.

"Something I had already," China said. I noticed how she brushed against Chip.

She and Chip were no longer being secretive about their relationship. They were very affectionate with one another in my presence. I kept drinking glass after glass.

"Chip, have you ever thought about doing a threesome?" I asked.

Chip looked at China before responding, "I've done it."

China placed her drink down and eased to the edge of the seat. "If your ass wasn't so drunk, I would make you go home."

"Calm down, girl. I was just asking. You, me, and Chip are chilling. You never know what's on a person's mind."

China stood and pulled me up. "I'm going to pretend like you didn't say that. Come on. It's time for you to go to bed."

I giggled as she led me to the guest bedroom. "This house is so beautiful. I could stay here for the rest of my life."

"I could too, but it's still not big enough for the both of us." China helped me get undressed.

"Thank you, China. You're so good to me." I got under the covers.

China stopped and said, "You're welcome. But if you ever make a pass at my man again, I will cut your ass. I mean that." She turned the lights out and closed the door.

I passed out as soon as my head hit the pillow.

The next morning I woke up with a huge headache and in a strange bed. It took a minute for me to realize where I was.

I went to the bathroom and freshened up. The smell of fresh coffee brewing greeted me the moment I stepped out of the bedroom. I made a beeline straight to the kitchen. My mouth dropped opened at what I saw.

China was seated on the counter with her legs gapped open. Chip was feasting on her pussy.

SWIPE

Moaning, China threw her head back. When she did, her eyes opened and she saw me standing in the doorway. She didn't stop. She closed her eyes. "That's it, big daddy. That's the spot right there."

Chip used her words of encouragement and continued to please her. I didn't move. I stayed glued in that spot, getting hornier and hornier. While watching Chip pleasure China, I reached my hand in my pants and eased my fingers into my pussy and started pleasuring myself. I stopped and went back to my room and closed the door. Then I lay back on the bed and rubbed my clit until I climaxed.

After I washed up, I remained in the guest room. I heard a knock.

"Come in," I said.

China opened the door. "So did that help you relieve some frustration?"

"You know you can be a real bitch sometime."

"Thanks. That means I'm living up to my reputation."

"You could have stopped when you saw me in the doorway."

"Last night you wanted a threesome, so you shouldn't have been offended by what you saw."

"Last night, my ass was drunk too," I responded.

"Just in case you don't remember our conversation. Remember this, don't ever proposition my man again."

"I didn't," I started to say but kept quiet.

"We're good. I know the liquor was talking and I must admit: Chip is one fine MF. If he and I weren't already fucking, I would want to fuck him too."

KAYENNE

"I don't even want Chip like that anymore," I responded as I got off the bed to look for my shoes.

"Your shoes are over there." China pointed to the corner of the room.

I slipped on my shoes.

She walked me to the door.

"Thanks for letting me spend the night. I never would have made it back home."

China hugged me. "That's what friends are for."

"Sorry, about last night."

"We cool. Just don't let it happen again."

CHAPTER THIRTY-FIVE
China

In a matter of minutes, things went from sugar to shit. I was at work when I received a text from Trina, and I sent her a quick one back. I needed her and Mia to meet me at my place later. We needed to hash out a few things.

The couple in front of me were overly excited about the possibility of buying their first home. I scanned their application and went through the usual spiel about what they should expect and when they should expect an answer.

"Your credit score is good, so you shouldn't have any problems getting the loan approved," I assured them.

We shook hands and they left out with my card. I closed the door. Our offices had see-through windows, but I still felt like I had a sense of privacy when I closed the door to block out the sounds coming from inside of the bank.

I did the paperwork that was required and the rest of my day went smoothly.

As closing neared, I turned off my computer and grabbed my purse. I didn't take a lunch, so I didn't see an issue with leaving thirty minutes early.

KAYENNE

"China, can I see you for a minute?" Mr. Belk asked.

Mr. Belk's office was the only office that didn't have clear walls. I followed him into his office. Two men were seated in front of his desk.

Mr. Belk closed the door behind us. "China, this is Agent Marks and Agent Williams."

They both stood up and extended their hands. I shook them, hoping they couldn't hear my heart beat a hundred miles per minute. Agent Marks was an African American male that stood at least four inches taller than me. He had a clean shaven head. Agent Williams was a Caucasian male that stood about the same height as Agent Marks. He kept his blond hair cut low.

"Have a seat," Mr. Belk said.

I sat in the chair on the opposite side of the agents.

"Mrs. Frasier," Agent Marks said.

"It's Ms. Frasier, but call me China," I responded.

"Ms. Frasier," Agent Marks said. "The reason Mr. Belk has called you in here today is because he assured us you could be trusted."

I tapped my foot, trying my best not to show nervousness. "I still don't understand."

Both pulled out their cards and handed them to me. "We work for the FBI. We're investigating a fraud case. Actually, multiple fraud cases, and some of the victims have accounts at this bank. We are already making sure there's no security breach. If you could think of anything suspicious that's happened within the last, say, three to six months, please let us know or let Mr. Belk know."

"Sure. If I think of anything," I replied.

I was dismissed and left out of the office feeling uneasy about things. I didn't just walk to my car, I sprinted. Also, I didn't breathe until I was on the main road headed home. I called Chip. "I think we have a problem."

He agreed to meet me at home. I paced the floor waiting on Chip, Trina, and Mia. I poured myself drink after drink. I felt like the walls were closing in on me. Chip rushed in and saw my physical state. He grabbed me by the waist. "Baby, take some deep breaths. You got to calm down."

I breathed in and out, in and out, until my pulse went to an even rhythm. Chip let me go and we both took a seat.

"What happened?" he asked.

"I only want to say this one time. So as soon as Mia and Trina get here, I'll tell you."

Shortly thereafter, Mia and Trina arrived. Chip let them in and they followed him into the den where I was seated nursing another drink.

"The Feds came to my bank today," I blurted out. I didn't even give Trina and Mia a chance to sit down before doing so.

"But you're here, so that means they don't know anything," Chip said.

"They even asked me for my help." I pulled out the two cards I'd put in my bra earlier.

Chip looked at the cards and then passed them around to Mia and Trina.

Mia said, "This is serious."

Trina said, "I'm out. I don't want nothing else to do with it. I got my kids to protect."

KAYENNE

Chip was the only calm person in the room. "Ladies, we got some unfinished business. We can't just up and stop our operation just like that. We got customer orders to fulfill and workers."

"Fuck that. Everybody working for us know that this shit could end any time. I'm not concerned about customers or workers. I'm concerned with my freedom," I blurted out.

"If the Feds was on to you, they wouldn't have asked for your help. If you play this smart, you can redirect them in another direction," Chip said.

Chip had a point. In all of the excitement, I wasn't thinking clearly. All I knew was I didn't want to go to jail. I was too pretty to go to jail. Jail was not for me no matter how I looked at it. How could I have gotten myself in this crazy situation? I blamed Gerry. If it wasn't for Gerry, I wouldn't have had a need to result back to some of my scandalous ways. Yes, Gerry was the problem, and instead of stealing from others, it was going to be a change of plans. We were going to hit the mother lode and steal from his ass.

CHAPTER THIRTY-SIX
Trina

I listened to China rant, but I sort of blamed her for what was going on. Wasn't nobody snooping at my job. Wasn't nobody snooping at Mia's. She should have been more careful. Now because of her carelessness, our freedom could be at stake.

When China finished her rant, I said, "I'm quitting my job and it's not up for discussion."

"Fine. We need to wrap this up anyway," China responded.

"It was fun while it lasted," Mia said as she poured herself a drink.

Chip stood up and looked at all three of us. "I'll start shutting the operation down, but we got to be careful on how we handle this."

China said, "All you have to do is tell folks the Feds are on us, and you ain't got to worry about it."

"Look. You handle your end and let me worry about how to handle this side of things. I got this."

I looked up at him. "I hope so. Because I can't have this get back to Dale."

"Let me see a picture of Dale."

I pulled out my cell phone and scrolled through until I found a picture. I handed my phone to Chip. "That's my baby."

Chip asked, "How you end up with that punk motherfucka anyway?"

"Excuse me." I placed my hand out for my phone.

"That nigga there used to hang out with your man." Chip looked at Mia. "And any friend of Tony's is an automatic enemy of mine." He handed me back my phone.

"I've met Dale. I don't remember meeting him," Mia said.

"You might not remember, but I know for a fact he did. I don't forget a face or a name."

"When I get back home, I'm going to ask him," I said.

"And you living with him? When I heard he was an officer, I had to laugh. I wish he would try to arrest me. I'd kill him or die trying," Chip said.

China asked, "What did he do to you for you to have such hostility?"

"He killed my brother." Chip turned his back toward us and walked a few feet away.

My hand flew up to my mouth. "How long ago was this?" I asked.

Chip still remained with his back turned. "We were in high school. We were in rival gangs. I didn't see him pull the trigger, but he was standing near my brother's body. Him and your punk ass husband." Chip turned and stared at Mia. If looks could kill, Mia would have dropped dead.

"But if you didn't see him shoot him, you don't know for sure."

"You're right. I don't, but he was there. And if he didn't do it, he knows who did."

"Why didn't you tell the police so they could investigate?" China asked.

"'Cause that's not how we do it in the streets. We handle things ourselves."

China attempted to comfort Chip. "You talk about me calming down. Baby, you need to calm down."

"I'm calm. I'm real calm. Your girl just needed to know who she's sleeping with."

"Chip, I'm sorry. I didn't know. But I love him and I don't think he's into that kind of life anymore. He's a cop."

"Please, some cops are more crooked than the crooks they call themselves arresting." Chip looked down at me. "All I'm saying to you is you need to know what kind of man you're messing with. You can stay with him. I don't give a damn. Just make sure you know who you're dealing with."

I listened to them all talk, but my mind was on the other side of town. Here I thought Dale was the best thing that could ever happen to me. Was he just like the rest of the men that had come into my life? I couldn't bring myself to believe that. Dale may have been a thug at one time, but the Dale I know now was far from it. Chip could hold on to the anger, and I can't really blame him because I would probably feel the same way, but that's Chip's beef with Dale. It didn't have anything to do with me.

I dropped Mia off at her new place and went straight to the house. The kids were already asleep. Once I checked on them, I went to the bedroom to spend some quality time with Dale. Before doing so, we needed to clear up a few things.

I'd showered and was now under the covers with Dale when I said, "I ran into one of your old friends or frenemies?"

Dale stopped rubbing my back. "Who?"

"I forget the name," I lied. "But he said, you used to hang out with this dude named Tony, or Big T is what they called him on the streets."

"Yeah, I know Big T."

I sat up in the bed. "When were you going to tell me?"

"I know a lot of people. I grew up in the Grove. Everybody knew Big T."

"Why do I feel like you're hiding something from me?"

Dale shifted his body where we were now face to face. "Can I trust you?" he asked.

"Yeah," I responded, as if he asked a dumb question.

"Remember, I told you I had something to tell you."

"But every time you get ready to, there's an interruption."

"Exactly. I was going to tell you I knew Big T, but it's not in the way you think."

"Then what is it?" If Chip was right, I had to think of an exit plan. I had to think of my kids.

"Big T's my half-brother," he blurted.

My mouth flew open. I wasn't expecting that. He continued on. "We have the same dad. Our dad was screwing our moms at the same time. T's only six months older than me."

SWIPE

"Damn. That's messed up," I responded.

"And, that's not it. I used to hang out with him, but I wasn't participating in the things he did. I just hung out with him to try to keep him out of trouble."

"Oh really now. That's not what I heard."

"Regardless of what you heard, that's the truth." Dale turned and placed his feet on the floor. His back was now toward me.

"Dale, don't walk out on me," I said.

"I'm not going anywhere. Something else I want to tell you."

"What?" I walked around to where he sat on the bed and I sat beside him.

"Tony left me with a couple of million dollars. Well, one for him and one for me. That's how I was able to buy this house. I couldn't afford this house on a cop's salary."

"Are you serious? So you got the money?"

Dale frowned. "Trina, what is it that you're not telling me?"

"Mia's been asking Tony about the money and he won't tell her. Wait a minute. Why haven't you helped Mia out? That's your sister-in-law." The more and more I learned about this. The more and more I realized I didn't know Dale as much as I thought I did.

"I begged Tony to let me help her, but he told me that Mia didn't deserve any of his money. He thought she was messing with that dude named Chip."

My mouth flew open. "Mia ain't fucked with Chip since she started messing with Tony. That's some bullshit there. She had to move. Almost got her car repo'd. She spent all of her money sending him money to put on his books, and he got access to a million dollars."

Dale grabbed my hand. "Calm down, baby."

"No. You don't know the things Mia's been through because of him."

"I told Tony to let me help her out though. I really did."

"Why didn't you tell me you knew Mia?" I asked.

"Because it would have led to this. I don't like keeping secrets from you, and that's why I'm telling you now."

"This is messed up. Mia's gonna be pissed when she finds out."

"Baby, what I just told you, it's got to stay between us."

"Yeah, okay," I responded.

"So baby, now you see why I said we don't have to worry about money. I got you. I shared this secret with you to show you how much I trust you."

"I trust you too," I responded as we hugged. I trusted him, but not enough to tell him what I had going on.

We cuddled in bed. As soon as I heard him snore, I reached on the side of the bed and got my cell phone. I made sure to block the light from the screen and sent Mia a text message. "I need to stop by after I drop the kids off at school tomorrow. It's urgent."

I shut my phone off and stared at the ceiling.

CHAPTER THIRTY-SEVEN
Mia

I couldn't sleep after Chip mentioned that Trina's man knew Tony. Later on that night I got a text from Trina. I tried texting her and calling her back, but she never responded. I was living in a better apartment, but I still had no peace of mind.

The next morning, I found myself posted at the window looking out. Trina's car pulled up. I waited for her at the door.

After the usual greeting, we both sat on the couch.

"Now what did you have to tell me?" I asked.

"I'm not supposed to say anything, so promise me you won't say anything to Tony?"

"I can't make a promise unless I know what it is," I responded.

"Promise me," she repeated.

"Fine." I wanted to know what she had to say, so I agreed.

"After Chip told us that Dale and Tony knew each other, I went home and confronted Dale about it."

"Did you ask him about the murder?"

"Don't interrupt."

KAYENNE

"Hurry up. This suspense is killing me."

"Dale is Tony's half brother."

I almost fell off the couch. "I have never *ever* seen Dale until I saw him with you," I said.

"I don't know nothing about all of that, but I do know what he told me."

"Tony ain't never mentioned anything about a half brother. He got a sister and that's all I know about. She and I can't stand each other."

"Dale ain't got no reason to lie."

"I'm not saying that he is, but I don't believe him."

"You might if you knew that Tony left the money with Dale to keep because he thought you and Chip were still messing around."

My mouth flew open to talk. Nothing came out. Silence. I opened my mouth up again. Nothing but silence. Finally, after getting over the initial shock, I asked, "Where is the money?"

"Dale has it and he's been wanting to help you out, but Tony told him not to because he felt like you were screwing with Chip while he was out hustling for bread."

"I haven't slept with Chip since the day I fucked Tony. Tony should know that. I didn't fuck another man until Tony got his ass locked up. Tony was the one always fucking with other bitches. Do you know how much I've sacrificed for him? Do you? I've been that ride or die chick who's spent her last dollar to make sure he had money on his books. I'm the one getting frisked and feeling violated each and every time I go visit him. Don't no woman like visiting her man in jail, but I do it. Let me not talk about the phone bill. Each one of those damn phone calls cost ten dollars. The phone bill costs more than my cell phone bill. I could go on and on, but I won't."

By now I'm crying and hyperventilating. Trina attempted to help me by rubbing my back. "Put your head between your legs."

I did as instructed. I counted to ten in my head and slowly sat back up. "I'm fine. I've been struggling and his half brother has had the money . . . even wanted to help me out, and the man that's supposed to love me wouldn't let him."

"Dale made me promise not to tell you, but you my girl and I had to."

"Trina, I promise I won't let Tony or Dale know I know. I'm glad you told me. Now I know what I need to do."

Trina stayed over to make sure I was going to be okay. I assured her that I would be. I would be eventually anyway. I felt like the biggest fool. Tony probably could sense something was going on because he called. I accepted the call because if I had anything to do with it, this would be the last call. He better make it count.

"Hey baby, I missed you. I was expecting to see you this weekend," Tony said.

"I expected to have some money too, but that never happened."

"Aw, here we go again. Are you going to ever get off that shit?" he responded.

"Tony, it's like this: You got three days to get me some money. I don't care how you do it, but I need to feel some greenbacks in my hand in three days."

KAYENNE

"Bitch, you've lost your mind giving me ultimatums."

"I got your bitch. I wasn't your bitch when you was fucking me. I wasn't your bitch when I was sucking your dick." He'd pissed me off.

"Calm down, baby."

"No, don't be trying to be all sweet now. Like I said, have some money in my hands in three days or else, you can expect to receive some papers from me."

"Mia, don't be going and doing anything stupid. You know I can't do that."

"If you truly love me, then you will. You talk about love in your letters. It's time to pay up or shut up. Show me the love and show me the fucking money. Three days."

I hung up on him because there was nothing else we needed to talk about. He could marinate on that. This was the first day toward my independence. Fuck him and his so called love. Love dissolved the moment I found out he'd lied to me. Love not only doesn't live here anymore. Love has left the building and if it returned, I'm shutting the door in its face.

SWIPE

CHAPTER THIRTY-EIGHT
China

I wasn't expecting Agent Marks to be in my office, but as I shifted my purse from one arm to the next, there he was seated across from my desk. I wanted to find out who let him in my office because I know when I left the day before, I locked my office door.

He stood up as soon as he heard me walk through the door.

"Agent Marks," I said as we greeted each other with a handshake. "Where's your partner?"

"He's around here somewhere."

"Give me a minute to put my stuff up and then we can talk."

Agent Marks pulled out a small steno pad. "Great. Take your time."

I used my key and unlocked the huge bottom drawer of my desk. That's where I kept important items that I didn't want anyone to see. I also kept my purse there during the day.

I punched in a code on my phone so my calls would no longer go straight to voice mail. I looked up at Agent Marks who seemed to be staring right through me. "How may I help you today?"

"I need to find out how much the loans were for these three people." Agent Marks slid the steno pad in my direction."

"That information is confidential. I'm not supposed to give that information out."

He retrieved a piece of paper out of his pocket and handed it to me. I read it. It gave him the authority to request the confidential information. I also saw my manager's signature on the form.

I handed the paper back to him and logged on to my computer. Once I accessed the information he needed, I printed it out and turned and handed it to him. "Anything else?"

"This will be helpful."

"If you need anything else, just let me know," I said.

Agent Marks stood up to walk out. He stopped and then turned back and came closer to my desk. "I do have one more request. Are you available for dinner after work? We're not supposed to fraternize while on a case, but you're absolutely beautiful. I would kick myself if I didn't at least try."

I smiled. "I wouldn't want you to get in trouble."

"I won't tell, if you don't tell."

I leaned back in my chair. "I'll think about it."

"Please do." He held up the printout I gave him. "Thank you for this."

He left out of my office thinking that he had a chance with me. Even if I wasn't dating Chip, Agent Marks wouldn't be in the running. He worked for the Feds and I didn't trust him. Any man I'm with I have to have some type of trust and respect for him.

SWIPE

I logged off the computer and then back on under one of my co-workers log-ins. Once I accessed Gerry's account, I wrote down some key information. I used my throw away phone to call the bank's phone number. I entered Gerry's account number. My first attempt for a pin didn't work. Gerry, as smart as he was, he was simple. I tried his mom's date of birth and it worked. I did a small withdrawal transfer to a prepaid debit card that I had setup under a fake name.

Happy with the quick transaction, I disconnected the call, called and checked the balance on the prepaid debit card. The transfer completed successfully. The balance on the prepaid card was now two thousand dollars. Money that Gerry wouldn't miss right away.

Too engrossed in my plot, I didn't hear Mr. Belk call my name the first few times. I jumped when I realized he was standing near my desk. Man, I hoped he didn't see the sheet of paper. I used my arm to cover it.

"Did you have any problems with that agent?" he asked.

"None at all. I gave him the information he wanted and he left."

"Good. I think we won't have to see them anymore. I hate that those people's identities were stolen, but there's nothing tying us with that. Them using the same bank is just a coincidence."

"That's exactly what I said," I responded.

"If either one contacts you again, be sure to let me know," Mr. Belk said.

"I sure will," I assured him.

Mr. Belk reached into his jacket pocket and handed me an envelope. "This is for your dedication to this branch. You've done an excellent job since you've been back."

"Thank you," I said, opening it up and counting 50 twenty dollar bills that added up to a thousand dollars. I knew he had an ulterior motive for handing me the money, but I didn't care.

"China, please keep this between us."

"Don't worry. It's nobody's business." I slipped the envelope in my purse.

He left out and closed my door. I would be making a deposit at another bank as soon as I got off work.

Again I worked through lunch, but it didn't do any good because I still ended up getting off late. By the time I finished processing the loans for that day, everyone had gone home except Mr. Belk.

I locked my door and headed to the side door entrance where I had to enter a code to leave. Loud voices stopped me in my tracks. I walked toward the voices coming from Mr. Belk's office.

There were two people talking. One of them was Belk, but I didn't recognize the other voice.

Belk said, "You need to make sure those agents don't find anything, and if they do, the information needs to disappear. I've worked too hard for them to destroy it."

The other man talking said, "I told you they won't find anything."

"They better not."

I hurriedly went back and entered the code to exit and practically ran to my car. Mr. Belk wasn't concerned about me or anything I was doing, because

SWIPE

he had his own thing going on. Now I worried about
the thousand dollars he just up and gave me.

KAYENNE

CHAPTER THIRTY-NINE
Trina

Tension between Dale and I escalated over the next few days. "I think I should find a place for me and the kids to move to," I blurted after he gave me the silent treatment.

"I don't want you to leave." Dale turned in bed to face me.

"I can be by myself and not have to deal with a man who doesn't want to talk to me."

"You betrayed me, Trina. I knew you must have told Mia because I got a letter from Tony."

"I told you, I don't know why Tony's contacting you about some money. It's a coincidence."

"I don't believe in coincidences."

I folded my arms. "Well, I do."

"Now he wants me to give her a few thousand dollars. Saying she's been tripping lately and that should be enough to calm her down."

I held both of my hands up in the air. "I told you Mia was tripping, so that's nothing new. You got to have more evidence than that to prove that I told Mia anything. You the cop. You should know that."

"Okay. Okay. Maybe I overreacted."

SWIPE

"You did, Dale. I would never betray your trust like that," I lied as I hugged him.

It had been three days since I felt Dale's lips on mine. He kissed me. We were just about to have sex when his phone rang. "Let it go to voice mail," I pleaded.

"Naw. That's Tony."

Tony's timing was off because I was horny and I needed to feel Dale inside of me now. While Dale answered and talked to Tony, I positioned myself on top of his dick. Dale's eyes widened. "Oh shit!" he said as I bounced up and down.

He did his best not to moan while on the phone. "Tony, I got this handled. But damn. Look, I got to go."

Dale threw the phone on the bed. I could hear Tony yelling. Dale didn't care, and I sure didn't care as he slipped one of my nipples in his mouth as I continued to ride him. We both cried out in ecstasy.

He flipped me over and started hitting it from the back, tapping one of my ass cheeks lightly. The slight sting made me wetter. Each time he penetrated me from the back, my body shook with desire.

"Whose pussy is this?" Dale asked.

"Yours," I said over and over.

My legs shivered as he pounded faster and faster on top of me. His body got stiff as he released his hot juices inside of me. We both collapsed on the bed and into each other's arms. That was the best make-up sex I'd ever had.

Dale dozed off to sleep. I got my cell phone and quietly went into the living room. I dialed Mia's number.

"Whatever you said to Tony worked. He told Dale to give you a few thousand dollars."

"I'm going to take it, but I'm still divorcing his ass."

"What? Are you serious?" I whispered.

"Yes. The money he gives me, I'm going to use it to pay for a divorce attorney."

"Girl, we can talk later. I just wanted to slip out and tell you that."

I turned and almost dropped my phone.

"Who was that?" Dale asked from the doorway.

"Nobody," I lied.

"Oh yeah, it was somebody."

"Fine. It was my girl Mia. I was calling to check on her."

"Trina, if our relationship is going to work, you need to stop lying to me. I'm not one of those other jokers you used to messing with. Now tell me the truth."

"I'm telling you the truth. It was Mia. See."

I handed him my phone and he actually checked the call log. He handed it back to me. "Why did you tell Mia what I told you?"

I opened up my mouth to lie but changed my mind. He wanted the truth, so I was about to give it to him. "Because she's my girl, and if she knew something like that about you, I would want to know."

Dale looked at me and said, "Finally, some honesty around here. Now was that hard to do? I don't know why you didn't admit it the first time. Putting us through all of this for nothing. All of this could have been avoided in the first place," he said as he went on and on.

SWIPE

I tuned him out as we both went back to the bedroom. All of the talk he did, didn't stop him from going down on me. I threw my pussy in his face to shut him up. He shut up and my pussy started talking back to him.

"Dale, baby, I can't take no more. I can't take no more," I repeated as he had my whole body shivering as if I were having a seizure.

I loved Dale but my loyalty would always lie with Mia.

KAYENNE

CHAPTER FORTY
Mia

Just like Trina had informed me, I got five thousand dollars delivered to me. I stashed the money in the hidden floor board I created. That same day I went to my part-time job. I had to meet Chip at the trap house so I could distribute the last of the stuff to the girls. As soon as I got off work I headed there.

Chip didn't say much to me while we waited. "How are things with you and China?" I asked.

"Our relationship is not up for discussion."

"No need to be snappy about it," I responded.

"Don't ask then."

"Where are these girls at? You told them to meet us here at nine and it's almost ten. I'm tired."

Chip laughed. "Girl, you don't do anything all day but run that mouth of yours. But then again, talking as much as y'all women like to would wear me out too."

"For the record, I worked today."

One of the boys Chip had working security knocked on the door and then came inside. "Man, I need to talk to you."

"Whatever you got to say, you can say it in front of her," Chip responded.

SWIPE

"Pookie just told me those two ratchets just got pulled over by the cops. We need to get the hell up out of here just in case."

Chip said, "What the hell you waiting for? Help me get this stuff out of here."

"What's going on?" I asked.

"You heard him. The girls got pulled over. I don't know what that's all about right now, and we don't have time to find out. We got these boxes. I need you to get the small stuff. My truck is still parked back there, so we can take it all through the back door."

In less than thirty minutes, all three of us had cleaned out the trap house. I hopped in the car with Chip and he dropped me off at my car that was on the next street. He waited until I was in my car and pulled off.

He went in one direction and I went in another. I thought I saw the girls in handcuffs standing outside of a patrol car when I passed by. It was. One of the girls looked toward my car like she recognized me. I hoped she didn't say anything. She didn't. She went back to talking to the officer. I looked in my rearview mirror and noticed them both getting in the back of the police car.

I called Chip and told him what I'd just seen. He said, "We all need to lay low for the next few days. Don't take any calls from them at all. In fact, take the battery out of the phone and get rid of it. Pronto."

I pulled over at the gas station and got out the other phone I used to take orders. In seconds I removed the battery from the phone and placed it in a bag. I got out of the car and pretended to be cleaning it out. Then I simply placed the bag in the garbage.

KAYENNE

A silver car pulled up. The window rolled down. "You moved on a brotha," Casper said.

"Call me." I got in the car. I wasn't in the mood to deal with Casper, but my body disagreed. Instead of waiting on Casper to call me, I dialed his number. "You want to hook up?"

"Why you think I've been looking for you? Where you live so I can follow you?"

"We can go to your place," I suggested.

"I got a roommate now," he said.

"Casper, I ain't got time to play these kind of games with you. Just say you got a woman at home."

"I do, but it's not what you think. I'll get us a room at Diamond Jack's"

I couldn't judge Casper on him stepping out, because when my heart was dedicated to Tony, I stepped out on him. I wish I had more self-control, but it was hard being a single married woman.

Two hours later, Casper and I were at the casino hotel fucking like rabbits. He hit every spot. The sheets were drenched with sweat from our wet bodies.

"Girl, if you weren't married, I would ask you to marry me," Casper said as he ran his hand through my hair.

"Please. You are not the settling down type." I didn't want to hurt his feelings and tell him he was too short for me. I only dealt with him because in the bedroom, height didn't matter.

Casper's phone kept ringing. "I hate to leave you like this, shorty, but if I don't get home, she going to keep calling me."

"I ain't tripping on that," I responded. "Handle your business. I'm about to jump in this other bed because these sheets are too wet for me to sleep comfortably on."

"So when will I see you again?" he asked as he bent and kissed me on my ass cheek.

"I'll call you."

"You better." Casper's phone rang again. He held up his finger to his lips to indicate he wanted me to be quiet. "I'm on my way home. I was handling some business."

I opened the room door. He kissed my nipple when he walked by, while still talking on his phone. Was he the kind of man I had to look forward to when I divorced Tony?

KAYENNE

CHAPTER FORTY-ONE
China

I watched Chip pace the floor. Ever since the girls he got working for him got busted last night, he'd been stressing. He kept me up all night. I was too tired to drag myself in to work, so I called in sick. Besides, I had to figure out what I was going to do after learning that Mr. Belk was doing some shady stuff at the bank.

"Chip, come on, baby. I fixed you a big breakfast. Come eat with me."

Chip ate his food in silence.

I started up the conversation and told him everything that happened at the bank. He said, "I think you need to go to lunch . . . hear me loud and clear. I said lunch, not dinner with that dude and find out what he knows."

"Oh, so you pimping now?" I asked.

"China, why you got to give me attitude every time I suggest you do something?"

"'Cause, I don't want to. The less interaction I have with Agent Marks, the better."

"Dude already attracted to you. All you have to do is flirt with him and ask him a few questions. He'll try to play big shot and end up telling you whatever you want to know."

SWIPE

I thought about it. Chip was right. I needed to know what he knew because right now, my nerves were on the edge.

"I'll do it. Let me call and see if he can meet me."

Four hours later, I was seated at Brothers Seafood across from Agent Marks eating shrimp étouffée. I closed my eyes as I savored the flavor of the scrumptious mouthwatering meal.

"China, is your mom Chinese?" Barry asked. Agent Marks insisted that I called him by his first name.

"No. Everyone thinks that. My mom's black and my father was white."

"Really, I never would have guessed. Normally when it comes to interracial relationships, it's usually the opposite." He took a bite of his hushpuppy.

"My parents loved each other, but things happen and me and my mom ended up here." I hadn't planned on divulging personal information to Barry, but I needed him to feel comfortable around me.

"So have you lived anywhere else besides Shreveport?" he asked.

"Yes, but I moved back. But enough talk about me. Tell me a little bit about you. How did you end up being an FBI agent?"

"Played cops and robbers as a little boy. Decided I wanted to be on the good side. Went to college and got recruited straight out of college."

"Interesting." I leaned over so he could see a little more cleavage. "Can you tell me what's going on with this investigation y'all got at the bank?"

Barry looked around the room. All the other patrons were all busy eating and conversing with their lunch mates. No one was paying us any attention. "I'm not supposed to be talking to you about a case."

"You weren't supposed to be asking me out, but you did."

"You got me there."

"Since I did agree to go out with you, you could at least oblige me with a little something something."

"Your branch manager should be relieved that we didn't find anything, so we have no reason to investigate further."

"Good. I mean, well good for the bank, but bad for us. Because all of the women enjoyed looking at two fine men on the premises."

"You can see me anytime you want. All you have to do is call."

"Oh really now."

"Yes, really." Barry licked his lips.

I squirmed in my seat as I imagined his lips on my lips in between my legs.

"Why don't we take a long lunch," he suggested.

"I'm not sure that's a good idea. My man won't like that."

"You failed to mention that," he said.

"Didn't think it was relevant. We were only doing lunch," I responded.

A waiter came up to our table. "Would you like some dessert? The cook just made a fresh batch of banana pudding and peach cobbler."

"Let me try that pudding," I said.

"Cobbler for me," he responded.

The waiter left and returned with our dessert. He seductively ate his cobbler. "Since I can't have you for dessert I had to settle for the second best thing."

"Agent Marks, you're really tempting, but I'm trying to be a good girl."

"Haven't you gotten the memo from Rihanna? It's time for good girls to go bad."

If you only knew, I said to myself as I ate my pudding.

He walked me to my car and held the door open. "If you ever change your mind, you got my number. I'm only a phone call away."

"I'll remember that," I said, right before getting in my car.

He tapped on my window. I rolled the window down.

"Are you sure there's something you want to tell me?" he asked.

"Nothing I can think of," I said, holding my breath.

He waved good-bye, but the look on his face indicated he wasn't buying my story.

KAYENNE

CHAPTER FORTY-TWO
Trina

I'd been hanging out with my girls all day. It had been awhile since I'd gone on a shopping spree. I was hanging stuff up in the closet when Dale walked in.

"Trina, what's all of this?"

"Clothes." I removed a few clothing items from a bag. "I bought you something too."

"Where did you get the money?"

"A student loan," I lied.

"But you're supposed to use that for school."

"I got enough to pay for my classes, but I also wanted to treat my babies. You and the kids."

"I like it, but baby, you ain't got to spend your money on me," Dale said.

"I know. But you've been so good to us. I just wanted to do something nice for you while I can."

Dale wrapped his arm around me and pulled me into a tight embrace. "You being here for me when I got shot was the nicest thing you could have ever done. You're the best thing that's ever happened to me."

We kissed and then I went back to hanging up clothes.

SWIPE

He stood in the doorway and just stared. "I sense something is wrong," I said.

"They suspended me for an additional two months. I got shot on duty. I almost died and they suspend me."

"Oh no, baby." I stopped what I was doing and gave him my full attention.

"After they investigated, they said I had no reason to shoot the perp. The fool shot at me first and that's why I shot at him. They aren't going to file any charges against me, but they said I could have used another way to detain him."

"That's crazy. What were you supposed to do? Let the man kill you."

"He almost did."

Dale looked a little down. He lay down on the bed. I got up and curled up with him. He didn't feel like talking, so we just held each other. We lay that way until we both fell asleep.

I woke up and Dale was gone. He left a note to let me know he took the kids to get pizza and that he didn't want to wake me since I was sleeping so peacefully. He was so sweet to me. I didn't know what I would do if I lost him.

On the evening news, the reporter came on the TV screen and said, "Sources tell us that two women detained last night might lead to further arrests. Officials thought it was a routine stop until they found false identification on each one of the suspects. If you think you have been a victim of identity theft, please call 555-1212."

The photos of two of the girls we'd been dealing with flashed on the screen. I dialed Mia's number.

KAYENNE

"Have you seen the news?" I asked as soon as she picked up.

"No need to. I've been laying low at this hotel. I'll swing by and we can talk there."

"We can't talk here. Dale might walk in on us. I'll meet you at your crib."

An hour later, Mia and I were pulling up to her apartment at the same time. As soon as we got inside, Mia told me about what happened the night before.

"I called Chip, but he hasn't answered his phone," Mia said.

"If those girls talk, all of us could go down." My worst nightmare was coming to life.

"I'm not even trying to think about that," Mia responded.

We both jumped when we heard a knock. Mia said, "That's probably China. I told her to meet me here."

China walked in and greeted us. She said, "The Feds won't be bothering us. They are moving on to something else."

I looked at Mia. Mia looked at me. We both looked at China. I asked, "Do you ever watch the news?"

"Yeah. Sometimes," she responded.

Mia blurted out, "The two girls Chip hooked us up with have been arrested. Chip didn't tell you?"

"Of course he did. Wait . . . Are you telling me they all on the news for a simple traffic stop?"

I said, "That's just it. Them bitches been snitching 'cause why are they saying that they could be part of an identity theft ring."

SWIPE

China pulled out her cell phone and dialed a number. We all could hear it ring because she put it on speaker phone.

"The block's hot so I'm going to have to call you back," Chip's voice rang out from the other end.

"Make it to Mia's. That's where we're camped out."

The call disconnected. We attempted to talk about other things, but each one of us was dealing with our own fears of being caught. I was thinking about my kids. If something happened to me, I didn't know where they would go. Dale cared about them, but he only did that because he knew my kids and I were a package deal. My cousin might take them in, but feeding three extra mouths for one or two days was nothing like feeding them every day.

Dale called me. I walked to the other side of the room to talk to him.

"I got your text. Are you still at Mia's?" he asked.

"Yes. She got a lot of stuff going on. Not sure of how long I'll be here. If it's too late, I might just spend the night."

"If it is, call me. I don't want to worry about you," Dale responded.

I hung up. How would this affect Dale and his job if I got arrested? Dale would never speak to me again, I'm sure. My mom used to pray all of the time. I found myself resorting to doing what she did. I closed my eyes and prayed to God to save me from the trouble I found myself in. I couldn't blame anybody but myself. Just because my girls were doing it, I didn't have to agree to participate.

KAYENNE

CHAPTER FORTY-THREE
Mia

I don't know why China and Trina were tripping. Those two ratchets knew that if they snitched, I'm the one they would come looking for, not them. We all jumped when we heard a knock on the door. Trina and China looked at me.

"It's your place. You answer it," Trina said.

I got up and walked to the door slowly. Another loud knock could be heard, and I looked through the peephole. I opened the door. "Dang, boy, you knocking on this door like you 5-0."

Chip rushed past me. I shut the door. He was drenched with sweat and sounded out of breath when he talked.

"Them ratchets got word to me that they want more money or they talking," Chip said.

I responded, "Maybe we should give them what they want."

"I don't trust that. It could be a setup," China said.

Chip added, "Exactly. The man I got on the inside told me the Feds supposed to talk to them, so this is serious."

"Chip, I didn't know you had a po-po on your payroll," I said.

"You ain't supposed to know. But I'm about to handle them two ratchets, so don't be surprised when you hear about it on the news."

"I wish you wouldn't have told me," China said.

"You got mad when Mia and I handled the other situation, remember? So now I'm telling you before it happens."

"What situation?" Trina asked.

"Nothing," Chip and I both said at the same time.

China stood up and went to Chip. "Baby, it's got to be another way. Don't you think harming them will bring even more attention?"

"Who said anything about harming them? The way to get a message to them is to harm one of their loved ones," Chip responded.

"I don't want to know anything else about it," I said as I put my hand over my ears.

Chip said, "I don't know what they've already told the police, so we definitely need to lay low for a minute. Baby, I'm going to need for you to start shredding stuff." He looked at me and then at Trina. "Put all the credit cards and IDs you got in a bag and dump them."

My cell phone rang. I answered.

"Is this Mia Jackson?" an unfamiliar voice asked.

"Who is this?" I blurted out.

"Is this Mia Jackson?"

I hung up the phone.

Somebody sounding like a white guy just asked for me by my full government name.

Chip said, "Give me all of the stuff you got now. Ladies, help her and then we all need to bounce."

I went to my closet and collected all of the identification cards and credit cards. They helped me put them in a department store bag.

Chip said, "I'll get rid of these. China, I'll see you at home."He left with the stuff and fifteen minutes later, China and Trina left.

Not even ten minutes later, I heard a loud pounding noise at my door. China or Trina must have forgotten something. I didn't expect to see two police officers staring back at me.

"Mia Jackson?"

"Yes," I said as I stood in the doorway.

"We need you to come down to the station. We have a few questions to ask you," the short female officer said.

"About what?" I asked.

"We can go more in details when we get you downtown."

"Well, I can't just leave my apartment unlocked. Can I at least get my keys?"

"Yes."

I started to close the door, but the male officer stopped me. "You'll need to leave the door open, so we can see you." Both of them had their hands on their guns that were still in their holsters on their side.

"My keys are right there." I pointed to the table.

I walked to the table. My cell phone was right next to it. I picked it up and slipped it in my bra without them seeing it.

"Follow us," the female officer said.

SWIPE

The male officer took my keys from me and locked my door. "I'll hold on to these," he said.

It was night time, so there weren't that many people out in the apartment complex. Fortunate for me because I hadn't been over here long and didn't need folks all up in my business.

The female officer opened the back of the police car. I got in. I'm just glad they didn't slap some handcuffs on me. They both got up front. The male officer drove. Their radio blasted. I noticed the male officer looking at me periodically through his rearview mirror.

From my position, I watched the rearview mirror and then removed the cell phone from my bra. I placed it down in my lap and alternated between watching the rearview mirror and the phone screen. I sent a short text to China: *Cops picked me up. On way to station.*

I put the phone back in my bra.

When we arrived at the police station, I could feel myself getting nervous. I wondered if this is how Tony felt when he got arrested. I had to remind myself that I hadn't been arrested, yet. That they just wanted to question me. But if all they wanted to do was question me, then why bring me down to the police station? Seems like we could have done all of this from my apartment.

I felt like a criminal as they led me down the hallway. Several people looked at us as we passed. They led me into a room with a table, one chair on one side and two chairs on the other. I'd seen enough TV to know that the glass that looked like a mirror was a two-way mirror where someone was on the other side watching.

I took a seat at the table as instructed.

The male officer said, "Someone will be in, in a minute to question you."

The female officer stood at the door as if she was guarding me.

"So can you tell me what this is about?" I asked.

"You'll find out soon enough," she said.

I tapped my foot. Nervous. I jumped in my chair when the door opened. A black man dressed in a suit walked in.

"Mia Jackson, I'm Agent Marks with the FBI. I have a few questions to ask you."

Shit just got real.

SWIPE

CHAPTER FORTY-FOUR
China

I couldn't leave Mia out to fend for herself. I had to do something. She needed a lawyer and fast. I called one of Gerry's friends and got a referral. I drove over the speed limit and made it to the police station to meet up with the lawyer. I waited until I saw the red SUV pull up. The red-headed woman got out and I knew she was the attorney. She'd described herself and she wasn't lying. Her fiery red hair was pulled back in a bun. Even though it was late, she was dressed in an off-white power suit with some red heels.

I got out of my car and walked up to her. "Ms. Monroe, I'm China."

She turned and greeted me with a handshake. "Call me, Becky. I promise to do what I can. I made a few phone calls on my way over, and it looks like they suspect your friend of fraud."

I had a blank look on my face.

"How well do you know Ms. Jackson?" Becky asked.

"She's a childhood friend."

KAYENNE

By now we're on the inside of the police station.

"I'm going to say you're my assistant. Don't say otherwise."

She walked up to the window and told the female officer, "I'm Becky Monroe and this is my assistant. I understand that you detained one of my clients, Ms. Mia Jackson."

The officer looked at the computer, and then a few minutes later she was escorting us down the hall. When we reached the last room, the officer stopped and knocked on the door. Another female officer opened the door.

"She's representing Mia Jackson."

We were allowed in the room. My mouth dropped when I saw through the clear glass Mia seated in one seat and Agent Marks seated across from her.

Becky said, "I need access to that room." She turned and looked at me. "You wait right here with the rest of these gentlemen."

I didn't feel comfortable in the room full of cops. My eyes locked with Agent Williams. He walked up to me and smiled. I didn't. He said, "Funny meeting you here."

"I could have gone another day without seeing you," I said.

"So are you friends with the lawyer or the suspect?" he asked.

"I didn't know she was a suspect. I was under the impression she was just down here to be questioned about something. Has she been arrested?" I looked him straight in the eyes.

"I can't discuss that with you. But you never answered my question."

"I'll answer yours when you answer mine," I responded, right before walking away and finding a seat.

I could feel his eyes on me. He took a seat a few seats down from mine as we all kept our eyes on the other room.

The sound from the other room was as clear as if we were right there. Becky introduced herself. She whispered something in Mia's ear. A look of relief crossed Mia's face. I could have sworn Mia looked directly at me.

I watched what happened as if it were on a movie screen.

Agent Marks asked, "Now that your attorney is here, would you please answer the questions now?"

Mia looked at Becky and then back at Agent Marks. "Sure."

"We have detained two individuals who both have mentioned your name. We need to know how do you know Shanequa Jenkins and Maria Perkins?"

"We're from the same neighborhood, so why wouldn't I know them?" Mia responded.

"They claim you are the person who gave them the false IDs."

"I don't know nothing about no false IDs."

Becky said, "Are you charging my client with something, Agent Marks?"

"Not at this time."

"Then this round of questions is over."

"I wasn't finished, Ms. Monroe," Agent Marks said.

"Unless you are charging my client with something, then yes, you are." Becky stared at Agent Marks without blinking an eye.

Agent Marks pulled out a business card and handed it to Becky. "As this investigation continues, I reserve the right to ask your client further questions."

"If the need arises, you're welcome to call my office and I'll make sure Ms. Jackson is available for questions."

A few minutes later, I met Mia and Becky in the hallway. I wanted to hug Mia, but refrained from doing so as I came face to face with Agent Marks.

I could tell he had a lot of questions, but I didn't wait to see what they were. Instead I followed Mia and Becky out of the police station. We stood near Becky's car.

"Mia, I want you to call me if they contact you again. In the meantime, I will be staying on top of this fraud case. China, we'll talk later."

Becky got in her vehicle and Mia and I got in mine. We both didn't say anything until we were out of the police parking lot.

"What do they know?" I asked.

"Not much. Those ratchets told them I gave them the ID cards."

That's not good. Not good at all. If they got evidence on Mia, then the trail could lead to me, and I wasn't about to be hauled off to jail. I didn't want to do it, but I had no choice. I called Chip's number. "Do it," I said.

No other words needed to be said. Chip knew exactly what I was referring to. I ended the call, sealing the death warrant on two individuals that had nothing to do with this case, but just got caught up because they were related to the wrong two individuals.

No one's safe on these streets when someone else's freedom was at stake.

KAYENNE

CHAPTER FORTY-FIVE
Trina

Dale wouldn't leave me alone long enough for me to dispose of the fake IDs and credit cards. I tried to get him to go to the store, but everything I asked him for he would locate in the house. Last night I barely slept after getting the call about Mia being questioned by police.

It was the weekend, so the kids didn't have school. I tried to pretend like I was listening to them as they talked to me over breakfast, but my mind was a million miles away. Dale had a huge fenced in backyard, so I made the kids go outside to play.

"Don't go out that gate, you hear me?" I said to Xavier.

I walked to the bedroom and Dale was in the closet. He walked out holding credit cards in his hands. "What's this?"

When I ran up to him and tried to grab them, he swung his hand so that I couldn't. "You had no business going in my stuff."

"I was looking for something. I didn't deliberately go in your stuff. But don't avoid the question."

"What it look like?" I asked, struggling with two emotions, anger and fear.

SWIPE

He poured out all of the contents in the bag onto the bed. He picked different ones up and started calling off names. He held up an ID. "The names are all different, but you know what's the same? Your pretty face."

I started breathing heavily. "Dale, it's not what it looks like."

"Oh, yes. It's exactly what it looks like. You're part of that identification theft ring my boys been talking about. Trina, why?"

"I don't know what you're talking about. I don't even know those girls."

He picked up a few of the cards in his hands. "How you going to lie to me in my face and the proof is right here."

"Please, let me explain," I begged.

"Go ahead. I want to hear this." Dale plopped down on the bed.

I stood in front of him. "I was two weeks away from being kicked out on the streets. If it was just me, then no problem, but I have three kids. The money I was making at the fast food joint wasn't enough to cover all of my bills. I didn't want to, but I felt like I had no choice. I needed the money to pay my rent. That's why I did it. I swear."

"But look at this." He pointed to the cards. "This is more than about paying your rent."

"I admit I got a little greedy but I stopped. I promise you I stopped. I got enough money saved and don't ever have to do it again."

"Damn, Trina, what am I supposed to do? I'm an officer. I'm supposed to uphold the law."

I blinked my eyes a few times. "Technically, you're not an officer, because you've been suspended for a few months, so you aren't under any obligations to turn me in."

"That's not the point. You've been stealing from people and that's just not right."

He walked out of the room. I rushed behind him. "What are you going to do?" I asked.

"I don't know." Dale went out the front door.

"Please don't turn me in," I begged.

Dale kept walking toward his car. I stood in the doorway and watched him peel out of the driveway burning rubber.

A few hours later, Dale still hadn't returned. Tears fell down my cheeks. I had to get myself together. I had to for the sake of my kids. I called Mia but got no answer. I called China and said, "Dale knows."

"Trina, you need to pack as much as you can, and you and the kids need to come to my place. The good thing about Dale is he doesn't know too much about me, or am I wrong?"

"You're right. He doesn't know your last name or where you live."

"Hurry up. We will talk more when you get here."

I gathered up as much stuff as I could and made sure I got all of the credit cards and fake IDs and put them in one of the bags too. I wrote Dale a note letting him know that I was moving out and would be back for the rest of my stuff later.

"Yas, make sure your brother and sister are in the car. I forgot something."

SWIPE

I went back inside to grab this other bag that I'd forgotten near the bathroom.

"Trina, what's going on here? The kids told me y'all were leaving," Dale said as he stood in the bedroom doorway.

"Dale, move. I got to go now."

"You're not going anywhere."

I put my hand on my hip. "You think I'm going to stay here so you can turn me in. You think I'm going to let you take me away from my kids. I don't think so. Move, Dale. Move 'cause I got to get away."

"I'm not going to tell, okay? I love you, and as long as you promise not to do it anymore, I'm not going to say anything."

"How do I know I can trust you? You're a cop. I shouldn't have gotten involved with you in the first place."

"That's anger talking. Calm down, baby girl. Please don't do this. Please, baby. We can work through this."

"You walked out on me, remember? Maybe this time apart will make us both think about if this relationship we have is worth saving."

"Where will you go?"

"I'm going to a friend's house."

"Mia's. Good, at least I know you'll be safe."

I let him continue to think I was going to Mia's. "I'll call you when I get settled in."

He looked at the empty bed. "Where are the cards?"

"None of your business. The less you know. The better."

KAYENNE

An hour later, Mia, China, and I were seated in China's living room. Each one of us had a drink in our hands.

I listened as Mia and China recounted what happened at the police station. China said, "I hope Chip's plan works, or else ladies, I think we need to prepare for the worse scenario."

"The lawyer you got me is a bad chick. She stood up to that agent like she would chop him up, eat him, and spit out his bones," Mia said.

"She came highly recommended. But let's hope we don't have to use her, again."

"I know that's right," I responded.

CHAPTER FORTY-SIX
Mia

It was something about the bed in China's guestroom that made me sleep like a baby. I don't know if it was the soft and firm mattress, or the fluffy pillows. When I woke up the next day I was fully refreshed.

I could hear Trina's kids playing in another room when I walked out in the hallway. Trina yelled, "Y'all stop that. You break something, your aunt China going to be mad and kick us out."

"Good morning," I greeted Trina.

She responded, "Good morning. China went to the store. She'll be back."

Trina and I were glued to the morning news. Nothing else was mentioned about Shanequa and Maria. I felt relieved. I was getting bored, so I went to the room to get my phone.

My cell phone rang. It was the number to the prison. I debated whether to answer it. I didn't feel like talking to Tony, especially after our last conversation. He called right back. This time I answered. After accepting the call, I regretted it.

"Mia, what's going on? I heard you were arrested," Tony said from the other end of the phone.

"Once again, your sources don't know what they're talking about."

"My sources know exactly what's going on. It was my brother."

I had to laugh. "So now you tell me about 'your brother.' Why now, Tony?"

"Because he told me everything."

"There's nothing to tell."

"Credit card . . . does that word mean anything to you?" he asked.

I paused. "Excuse me."

"I won't say nothing else just in case they listening in on this call. But I instructed my brother to give you some money for a lawyer."

"No need to. I got one."

"Who?" he asked.

"Becky Monroe," I responded, as I sat on the edge of the bed.

"She's good but expensive. Who you been fucking to pay for her?"

"Who I'm fucking is no longer your concern," I responded with a slight attitude.

"As long as you're my wife, it will always be my business."

"Speaking of that. As soon as they can draw the papers up, you should be receiving some papers."

"What kind of papers, Mia? I know you ain't trying to divorce me. I'm not signing shit," he said.

"Fuck you, Tony. I've been by your side through thick and thin, but you left me out here on these streets. I'm in this situation because of you. If anything happens to me, it's all your fault. Believe that."

Tony whined from the other end. "I'm sorry. I made a mistake. I thought you was still messing with ol' boy. That's the only reason. I didn't want you spending my bread on him."

"You didn't trust me because your ass was the one always creeping. But me, I was that stupid wife. Regardless of the late night phone calls, or the bitches looking at me sideways in public, I ignored all of that and chose to stay with you and was faithful the whole damn time."

The operator interrupted and said we only had a minute left on the call.

"Mia, baby, I love you. I promise I'll make it up to you."

"I love you too, but Tony, it's too damn late."

The call disconnected. I didn't realize tears were flowing down my face until after the call ended. I went to the bathroom and washed my face. As I stared at myself in the mirror, I didn't like what I saw. My eyes were red and puffy. I looked in the medicine cabinet and found some eye drops.

China had returned by the time I went back into the other part of the house. I heard her and Trina talking from the kitchen, so I went to join them.

"I came to tell you I was back, but I could tell you were in a heated discussion," China said as she put away some of the groceries she had in the bag.

"That was Tony. I told him I was divorcing him and world war three broke out."

"I'm glad you're finally dropping that dead weight," China said, without stopping what she was doing.

I turned toward Trina. "Dale told Tony I knew everything."

Trina rolled her eyes. "I'm not surprised. Dale's upset that I left him."

"Tony tried to explain himself, but it still don't make sense to me. He acted like we were this happy couple, but the whole time he's thinking I'm messing over him with Chip."

China stopped doing what she was doing. "Say what?"

"Trina didn't tell you?"

"No, she didn't." China looked at Trina.

"Didn't feel it was my place to say anything," Trina said in her defense.

China used her hands to talk. "So what is it no one's telling me?"

I sat down on a bar stool. "The reason Tony wouldn't tell me where the other money was is because he thought I was still messing around with Chip."

"When was this supposed to happen?"

"This was when he was still on the streets. All of this time, I've been struggling because of his own insecurities."

"If he loved you, he wouldn't have left you to fend for yourself, is all I'm saying. Just like my bastard of an ex-husband. But his ass is paying big time. I hadn't told Chip this because he would be pissed, but I've been having money transferred from Gerry's account to a few prepaid cards. By the time they are able to trace them, I will have withdrawn the cash."

SWIPE

China don't play. She was going to get her money from Gerry one way or another.

KAYENNE

CHAPTER FORTY-SEVEN
China

Xavier walked into the kitchen. "Uncle Chip wants you."

"Thanks, baby."

Trina said, "Go ahead and see what he wants. I'll cook up something."

Mia rubbed her stomach. "Good, because I'm hungry."

Chip was upstairs in the bedroom packing clothes when I located him. "Baby, what's going on?" I asked.

"There's a warrant out for my arrest."

"For what?" I asked.

He stopped packing and looked at me. "What you think? Those ratchets gave up my name."

"I thought you were going to take care of them."

"I waited. I waited because of you and your conscious and now this shit. I got to get out of town and quick because I'm not going to jail."

"Hold up, now. This ain't my fault. You should have made sure you chose people who could be trusted. Not my fault you chose two snitches that will drop your name at a dime."

SWIPE

Chip didn't say anything. He went to the bathroom and came back out with his razor and other items. "Don't nobody know where you stay. I don't even mention your name to anybody I deal with, so you should be safe. I will call you from a new number once I get settled."

"If nobody knows you're here, why don't you just hang out here for a few days? Trina and Mia are hiding out here."

Chip stopped and turned to face me. For the first time, I could see fear in his eyes. "You might be right. Let me go out and change the plate on my car just in case a police cruises down this street and run it."

"Baby, this is not the hood. They don't do that around here."

"I'll be back."

"I'll unpack your stuff."

"No, leave it. I still haven't decided on if I'm staying or how long I'm staying."

I didn't know what to do. Chip had a warrant out for his arrest. Mia's been questioned. Things were going from bad to worse. Chip remained and when Monday morning came, I started to call in sick. Chip said, "No, you need to go in. Right now, nobody knows you're connected to me. Keep up your normal routine."

I ran into Trina downstairs. "Where are you going?" she asked.

"To work."

"Anything you need me to do while you're gone?" she asked.

"Yes. Keep an eye out on Chip for me. If he leaves the house, text me."

KAYENNE

The first part of my morning at work went like it normally does. I had a few meetings with clients, and I usually worked through lunch, but needed a breather. Besides, I wanted to check on things at the house.

While walking to my car, I looked through my purse for my keys. I wasn't paying attention and walked into someone.

"Excuse me," I said as I recognized Agent Marks.

Agent Marks said, "Get in and drive."

I unlocked my door and he got in the passenger side. "Why are you stalking me?"

He laughed. "I'm the one who asks the questions."

"What do you want with me? I thought the bank investigation was over."

"It's been re-opened and I think you know why."

I almost hit the car in front of me at the light because I was looking at Agent Marks. Our bodies jerked when I slammed on the brakes, avoiding a collision by a few inches.

"I don't know what you're talking about."

"The two young ladies we arrested had identification that matched the information we requested from your bank. I find out that you're working with the attorney whose client is one of the ladies that was fingered by one of the suspects. You work at the same bank."

I had to think. I had to think fast. Everything pointed toward me, but I refused to go down for it. I interrupted him. "I get it. All of those are coincidences."

SWIPE

"I've come to learn that there are no such things as coincidences. The facts are there. Do I need to go any further?"

I pulled the car over into a grocery store parking lot and parked. A quick shift to the right placed Agent Marks and me face to face. "I do have something to tell you, but I was afraid to before. If I tell you, you have to promise me that nothing will happen to me."

"Without me knowing the information you are about to disclose, I can't make those type of promises."

I turned the engine back on. "Then Agent Marks, there's nothing else we need to talk about." I reached for the gear. He placed his hand on top of mine to stop me. "Fine. What do you know?"

"Will you be able to protect me?"

"I won't let anything happen to you unless you're part of the problem."

I crossed my fingers out of his sight. "I can promise you I had nothing to do with what I'm about to share with you. What I will tell you will not only jeopardize my job, but possibly my life."

Agent Marks pulled out his tape recorder. "I'm ready."

"No. Tape. I will only talk off record."

He turned the tape recorder off and placed it back in his jacket pocket.

I continued. "I overheard Belk talking about stealing money."

I recounted to Agent Marks what I heard. I even added some things so it would look like Belk was even a part of the identity fraud case he was working on.

"Is he aware that you overheard him?"

"No. If he did, do you think I would be here talking to you?"

"I'm going to get out here. I'll have someone come pick me up. Go back to work and act normal. I'll be in contact."

"What's going to happen next?" I asked.

"We're going to take Belk down. This time he won't even see it coming."

Agent Marks slipped out of the car without saying another word. I was in a daze as I drove back to work and went to my office. The rest of the day I was on automatic pilot.

When I got back home, I felt the bottom drop out of my heart.

Waiting on my pillow was a note from Chip:

Sorry, babe.

I will call you as soon as I can. I love you more than life itself.

Be sure to do what we discussed. The time has come.

SWIPE

CHAPTER FORTY-EIGHT
Trina

After I dropped off the kids at school, I decided to swing by and see Dale. He was sitting on the couch watching TV when I entered. He got up and hugged me and held me tight. "I've been worried about you."

"I'm all right."

"We need to talk." He grabbed my hand and led me to the couch.

We both took a seat. He brushed my hair out of my face and said, "I'm not going to turn you in."

"I have my doubts," I said.

He placed his hand on my cheek. "Do you know how much I love you?"

"I thought I did, but the way you acted with me yesterday, I couldn't tell."

"I was upset. You've been doing stupid stuff. I don't want you to end up in jail. I'll lose you. The kids would lose you."

I tried to control the tears, but they wouldn't stop falling from my eyes.

Dale wiped my face with his hand. "Don't cry. We're going to think of a way to make sure you don't have to see the inside of a jail."

"That's one promise you won't be able to keep. I have a confession to make. Those two girls have snitched on two of my friends that I've been working with."

"I got enough money that you, me, and the kids can move. We'll move to California."

"I can't just up and leave. What about my friends?"

"What about them? I know enough about Mia to know she would leave. And that other chick you talk about all of the time. What's her name?"

"China."

"Yeah. She had no problem leaving before from what you said, so what makes you think she wouldn't leave again? Then you're left here to deal with the aftermath. I'm not about to let that happen. Not on my watch. I'm already making preparations."

"Dale, if it's tied back to me, there will be a warrant out for my arrest. Me leaving is not going to solve the problem."

"I looked at the IDs. You're good at changing your appearance. That's all you will have to do."

"What about one of your neighbors? They'll snitch, and then you'll be guilty because you ran away with me."

"My neighbors keep to themselves. They know the kids, but if I asked them how you looked, they probably couldn't give a good description."

"I don't know. I'll have to think about it."

"So I should expect you and the kids back home today, right?"

"No. I think me being where I'm at is best for now. Until I decide on what I want to do next."

"Come home. That way I can protect you. I'm packing and I'm going to make the arrangements. By the end of this week, we need to be pulling out."

"Dale, I told you, I'll think about it. I can't make you any promises."

He didn't want me to leave, but after packing a few more clothes, I left.

China's front door was unlocked when I returned so I walked in the house and yelled, "I'm back."

I didn't get a response. I walked past the living room and stopped when I heard Mia's voice.

"Tony, I need that money so I can get out of town." Mia paused and then she continued. "Fuck China. Trina got Dale. She'll be all right."

So Dale was right. Mia wouldn't hesitate to leave me in the trenches. I heard all I needed to hear. I knew now that I had to make some plans of my own. It was each man, or in this case, woman for herself.

I pulled out my phone and called Dale. "Baby, I'll do it. I'll stay here for a few days, and then we can head on out."

"You sure?" he asked.

"Positive. You and the kids are my world. Y'all are my first priority."

"Come home tonight."

"No. Got some things I need to clear up here before I go."

"Don't tell anyone what we plan on doing," Dale said.

"You don't have to worry about that. They will find out when they come looking for me."

"I didn't know you were back," Mia said from the doorway.

"I got to go. I'll talk to you later." I hung up the phone with Dale and addressed Mia. "I yelled out, but you must didn't hear me."

"I was on the phone talking to Tony," Mia responded.

"Really?"

"He claims he's going to ask Dale to give me some more money."

"For what?" I asked, already knowing why.

"I need to lay low for a minute. I don't even want to go back to my apartment. I'm afraid the police may come back again."

"So you going to stay here? You can't keep hiding out, you know."

"I'm going to move around," she said.

"Like where?"

"It's best that you don't know," she responded.

"Oh, so you're going to bounce and leave us here to clean up the mess."

"If Dale gives me enough money, maybe I can send for you and the kids once I get settled."

"That's okay. I'll take care of me and mines."

"Whatever. You ain't got to have an attitude."

"I can't believe you. You're *supposed* to be my girl. You were going to bounce without even telling me."

"No, that's not true. I was going to tell you. Just not tell you exactly where. I don't even know where yet."

"Are you sure you didn't tell the police anything the other night?"

"Trina, you know me better than that. You know I would never snitch on my friends."

SWIPE

"I used to think I knew you, but now . . . I just don't know."

KAYENNE

CHAPTER FORTY-NINE
Mia

Trina's been having a funky attitude with me ever since she's gotten back here. She's got a man. Let him take care of her. I'm out here on my own. I got to take care of me. I'm the one who should have a funky attitude. I'm the one the cops questioned. I'm the one whose life they're probing into.

My cell rang again. It was my supervisor. I forgot to call in. I answered as if I'd been sleep. "Hello." I made the "o" drag.

"Mia, where are you?"

"I wasn't feeling too well. I just woke up."

"You know what. Don't bother about coming back in. You've been doing a lot of that lately, and frankly, you are not dependable."

"But . . ." I said as if I really cared.

"You can pick up your last check Thursday."

I didn't want to go back to that job anyway. As I went into the kitchen, I decided to cook a nice dinner for all of us. I heard the front door close and I went toward it to peep out. Trina was getting in her car to leave. I locked the door.

By the time China got home, I'd finished cooking.

"Something smells good up in here," she said as she walked in the kitchen.

"I hope you don't mind. I cooked a roast and some mashed potatoes."

"You can almost cook better than me," she said as she got a spoon and sampled my whipped up garlic mashed potatoes. "Love it. Where's Trina?"

"She probably went to pick up the kids," I responded.

"It don't take that long to pick up some kids and come back."

"I will call her. On second thought, she probably won't answer the phone when I call. You call her," I said.

China pulled out her phone from her purse and dialed Trina's number. "Where you at? Call me." China looked at me. "Getting her voice mail."

"Chip hasn't been here all day. You heard from him?" I asked.

"No. He's gone."

"What do you mean gone?" I sat down on the bar stool.

"He left."

I found myself getting real upset. "He can't just up and leave like that. He was an important part of our operation. We don't know who all he's talked to. Who all he's been paying. What are we going to do?" I said.

China ran her hand through her hair. "I talked to that FBI agent that interviewed you."

"Did he come up to the bank?" I asked. If he was following China, then he knew we could all be tied together.

KAYENNE

China explained what happened and how she knew him. "So I'm trying to fix it so they will look at Belk and not me. He's done it on other accounts, so they might as well group them all together."

I agreed. "Then we shouldn't have anything to worry about." I felt a little better knowing that.

"How long you plan on staying?" China asked.

"I'll be gone by the end of the week."

"You can stay as long as you want, but I plan on taking a trip this weekend, so I just wanted to know your plans."

Little did China know, I'd planned on leaving to go out of town this weekend myself, but never to return.

After she and I ate, I decided to go to my apartment and get some important items that couldn't be replaced. I borrowed one of China's cars since mine was still at the apartment complex. Everything else could stay put. I'd paid up my apartment for six months, so there was no need for anyone to go in or out of my place.

The parking lot was full, so I ended up parking several doors down from my apartment. Everything was safe and secure. I grabbed a suitcase and packed enough clothes to last me for at least a week. Then I retrieved the money out of the floorboard and placed it under my clothes in the suitcase.

Once I located my purse and some pictures of family and went to the door, I turned to make sure I hadn't forgotten anything. My cell phone rang as I was reaching for the door.

"Where you at?" China asked from the other end of the phone.

SWIPE

"I'm on my way back now," I responded.

"Just checking."

"I'll be there soon, so no need to worry about me."

We ended our call. I pulled up the handle on the suitcase and rolled it down the stairs.

"Mia Jackson!" a man called out.

I turned, and out of nowhere the jump out boys and a few police officers in uniforms and black coverings over their chests appeared.

While staring at several guns, I dropped the handle on the suitcase. My purse slid off my shoulder as I placed my hands in the air.

One of the officers walked up to me. "Mia Jackson, you're under arrest for fraud. Anything you say can and will be held against you in a court of law." I heard him recite my Miranda rights. Everything was moving in slow motion.

The parking lot became like Grand Central Station. All of my neighbors were either outside, or on their balconies looking at me being taken away in handcuffs.

One of the officers pushed me in the back of the police car. I tried not to cry, but it was hard not to. I looked back up at my apartment and at the many faces staring back at me as the police car drove way. I woke up a free woman, but I was going to bed behind bars not knowing when I would ever go home.

KAYENNE

CHAPTER FIFTY
China

Worry filled me as I waited and waited for Trina and the kids to return. I even called Trina several times but still didn't get an answer. Where was she? I sent her a text message to call me.

Becky's number displayed on my cell phone. "I just received a call from the city. Your friend Mia has been arrested. Are you going to pay me to represent her?"

"No. I will no longer be needing your services."

"That's all I needed to know. I will let her know she will need to find another attorney. If there's anything else I can do for you, call me. You've got my direct number."

"I sure will." I hung up the phone.

In war, there had to be some casualties. Mia was just a casualty of war. I wasn't worried about her snitching because she knew the rules of the streets. Besides, she was on the front lines. She knew the risk involved when she agreed to be the one to order and hand out the stolen merchandise.

My house phone rang. I wasn't familiar with the local number, so I answered. "You have a collect call from an inmate. Mia's voice came through and then the recording continued. To accept press one. To block all calls from this facility press five."

My finger was on the five, but instead I pressed the one. "Thank God you answered," Mia said.

"What happened?" I asked.

"I was leaving the apartment and there were like a gazillion police there."

"What are they charging you with?" I asked, although I already knew.

"Identity theft, forgery, defrauding the post office. A whole bunch of shit. Some stuff I didn't even do."

"Damn. Well, hopefully your lawyer can work something out."

"That's why I'm calling. Ms. Monroe said she couldn't represent me. Can't you call her and talk to her?"

"I can, but she has the right to refuse clients, so that's out of my control."

"So you mean I got to sit up here in jail. I can't afford a lawyer."

"You should be able to get a court-appointed one when you go to your bail hearing."

"You two-faced bitch! So you're not going to help me?"

"I'm going to call around, but my money situation is looking funny too."

"What about the money from your ex? Can't you get something from him and help get me a lawyer. You know how these janky court-appointed lawyers are."

"I'm going to look into it, but in the meantime, you need a lawyer."

"Fine. Can you at least send me twenty? Well, it got to be a money order. I got here for dinner, and the mess they gave us I wouldn't feed to my dog."

"I'll call back up there tomorrow to get the address. Don't worry, it's going to be all right," I said.

The phone call ended. I hung up.

Hours later, Trina still hadn't returned and hadn't responded to any of my messages.

I turned on the ten o'clock news to see if Mia's arrest would be mentioned. When I saw her mug shot appear on the screen I turned up the volume. "Mia Jackson was arrested earlier today. She's said to be the mastermind behind the credit card and identity theft ring that took place right here in Shreveport. Be sure to go to our website for more information about this ongoing case and others. Now back to you, Bill."

I laughed out loud. "Mastermind, *please*." But as long as they thought she was the ringleader, then nobody would be coming after me.

I saw Chip's photo on the screen. "This just in. Authorities are looking for this man. Chip Harvey. He's connected to the same case. Police believe he's hiding out in the Hollywood area where he's known to frequent. If anyone knows of his whereabouts, a ten thousand dollar reward has been offered."

I used my phone and took a snapshot of the screen.

Wherever Chip was, I hoped he was out of Shreveport. I still hadn't heard from him, so I was a little worried.

SWIPE

An hour later I dozed off on the couch. My lower back ached when I woke up the next morning. I showered and dressed as if it were just a normal day. Everyone at the office seemed to be in a jovial mood. Everyone except Belk.

"Good morning, Mr. Belk." I spoke to him and he grunted instead of giving me a hello. I watched him go back in his office and close the door. He thought he was having problems now, just wait until the Feds came after him.

I was barely there a good ten minutes when my phone rang. "This is China, how may I help you?"

"It's me," Chip responded.

"Hold on a minute." I got up and closed my door. Then I sat down and picked up the phone. "I'm back. Where are you?"

"I can't tell you that. Are you doing what we planned?"

"Yes. One down. Don't know where the other one is at."

"Meet me at the designated place. Leave tonight."

"Tonight. I'll leave in the morning."

"China, listen to me. You need to get out of there and leave no later than tonight."

"Fine. I planned on putting in my notice Friday. I'll just give it to him today." While talking to him, I retrieved an envelope out of my purse with my resignation letter and placed it on my desk.

"My source inside tells me Mia's facing a lot of charges. It'll be years before she gets out. If she gets out."

"You don't think she'll say something."

Chip interrupted me. "Even if she does, we'll both be long gone by then."

"I see my friends from the FBI are here. I guess Belk is about to get his."

"That's all I needed to hear. I'm out. Love you."

"Love you too," I responded as I watched Agent Marks and Agent Williams go to Mr. Belk's office. I opened my door so I could hear but couldn't hear anything. Belk's office opened up. All three of them walked out. I guess they weren't going to embarrass Belk by making him wear handcuffs. I pretended to be busy and shifted papers on my desk.

Agent Marks appeared in front of me. "China."

I looked up. "Hi, Agent Marks. You're back."

"Yes, and it's unfortunate too."

From behind Agent Marks, I could see Belk being handcuffed by Agent Williams. "So you got him?" I asked.

"China, can you come with me?" he asked.

"I don't want him to know I told you anything. He might send some bad people after me."

"He's not concerned with you, but we are."

"Excuse me?"

"China Frasier, you are under arrest for bank fraud. I need you to come with me."

He recited my Miranda rights, but I was so in shock that he was arresting me that I heard him but didn't hear him.

"You've made a mistake," I said, staying glued in my seat.

"There hasn't been a mistake."

"I'm not working with Belk."

SWIPE

"We know. You got your own thing going on. One of the ladies at the restaurant we went to was able to positively ID you. It just took us this long to build a case."

My mouth dropped open in disbelief. The other bank employees were already mumbling, watching Mr. Belk being escorted out, but they practically screamed when they saw me being escorted out right behind him. I heard one of them say, "I knew she was up to no good, the first time I met her."

I turned and gave her a look when I walked by. If looks could kill, that bitch would be dead on the spot.

KAYENNE

CHAPTER FIFTY-ONE
Trina

Dale and I were now on the open highway. We were on I-20 westbound headed toward Dallas. The kids were in the backseat asleep.

Dale held my hand while he drove. I looked out the window. "You all right?" he asked.

"Yes. Thanks for getting Mia that lawyer."

"I heard Ms. Monroe was the best, and besides, she's not just your friend. She's my sister- in-law."

"Tony's not so bad of a dude after all," I said.

"Tony doesn't know."

"I'm glad Mia called and warned me. I never thought China could be so shiesty."

"Just because she lived in that big old house on the lake doesn't mean she didn't have ratchet tendencies," Dale said.

"I never told you where she lived," I said.

"You didn't have to. As soon as I found out what you and your friends were up to, I made sure I checked out China. Her refusing to pay for Mia's lawyer let me know that if she could do that to Mia, there's no telling what she would do to you."

"I got rid of my cell phone. I saw she was blowing it up."

"Baby, she thought you were dumb. She tried to take advantage of you."

"Yes, she did. But who outsmarted who?" I smiled for the first time since finding out Mia was in jail last night.

"We'll stay at the hotel tonight and then get back on the road in the morning."

"California, here we come," I said.

"Let's hope your girl China don't open her mouth. For now, you're safe."

Any other time I would be sure China wouldn't, but the way she did Mia, I wasn't so sure about anything anymore.

"What's going to happen to Chip?" I asked.

"I hate you walked in on that conversation," Dale said.

"Chip will probably get no more than two years for cooperating. Your girl didn't have any idea that Chip was working with us."

"He loved China. I can't see why he turned on her."

"He loved his freedom more. They got so much evidence on him that he could be locked up for sixty years if they charged him with it all."

"But dang. China trusted him."

"You and Trina trusted her and you see where Mia is."

I shook my head in disbelief. "It's still hard for me to believe China did this. The whole thing was her idea in the first place. She set us both up."

"She'll have plenty of time to think about it. Oh, I got something for you. It's a gift from Chip. Check my wallet."

I opened up the wallet. I pulled out the ID that had my face on it. I saw that the name was different."

"California issued. Instead of Katrina, your name is now Katherine."

"My great grandmother's name was Katherine."

I took the fake driver's license and put it in my wallet right in front of my real one. I leaned back on the seat and fell asleep.

It took us two days to make it to the California state line. When we did, I jumped out of the car and stood in front of the sign. Dale took my picture.

Dale rented us another room. "This will be our home until I can find us a place."

"I love it," I said.

Xavier and Yasmin started jumping on the bed. "Wee!" Xavier said.

"Y'all both need to quit. Sit down somewhere."

"Oh yeah, baby, you're going to have to hurry up and find us a spot."

"I'm going downstairs to get some ice. You want anything?" Dale asked.

"I've been feenin' for some chocolate."

"I got your chocolate," he responded.

"Dale, not in front of the kids."

"I'm just saying." He teased me some more and then left us alone.

Dale's phone rang. I looked at the door and then got up to pick it up from the other side of the bed. I answered, "Hello."

"Put Dee on the phone," a male voice said.

"He's not here," I responded.

"I ain't got much time. Tell him Big T said he can run but he will find him."

"Who is this?"

"Don't worry about that. Just deliver the message."

The phone call ended.

I slipped on my shoes and ran down the hallway. Anxiously, I pressed the down button on the elevator. It was taking too long. I tapped my foot, still nothing. I looked for the stairway door and I rushed down the steps. The door was hard to open but I finally got it open. I went into the lobby.

"Where's the ice thing?" I asked the hotel clerk.

"It's not working," he said.

"Did a man about this height come down here asking for some ice?" I asked, using my hand to indicate Dale's height.

"Yes. He sure did. He said he was going down the street to the convenience store."

I rushed out the door and I saw the SUV still parked, so I ran to it. A man's limp body was beside it. Blood trickled down his head.

I felt a hand go over my mouth and I kicked and tried to scream.

"Baby, it's me," Dale said. He let me go and held me.

"What happened?"

"This fool tried to jack me."

"Is he dead?" I asked.

"Go get the kids and meet me at the side entrance."

"What about him?" I looked down at the body.

"Trina, we ain't got time for a long conversation, just do what I told you."

KAYENNE

Fifteen minutes later, we headed out on the road. When the kids fell asleep, I told him about the phone call.

"No wonder he looked familiar." Dale sped up. "I need to get that sim card out of my phone and then we can dump it."

At the next stop, we did just that. He filled up the truck with gas and I dumped the phone in the women's bathroom trash can.

Dale jumped on the open highway, destination unknown. All I knew was my man, my three kids, and I were safe for now and to me that's all that mattered.

SWIPE

CHAPTER FIFTY-TWO
MIA

They made me remove my tracks from my head. My hair was still long without them but just not as full. It's not like I needed to look good anyway. I was surrounded by nothing but women. They moved me from the city jail to the parish jail. After being searched and violated by the prison guards, who I seriously felt like they got their rocks off by frisking us in places that no other person's hand should go, I was issued some underwear, a bar of soap, tube of deodorant and an orange jumpsuit. I put on the clothes and five other women and I followed the prison guard to our cells. We heard cat whistles as we walked by. I ignored them and went inside my designated cell. The prison guard said, "You're fortunate. You got a cell to yourself. But don't get used to it. We'll be bringing some more in later."

I was going to enjoy it while I could. There was a sheet and pillow on the bed. It was better than what was at the city. Not home, but it would be home until I went to court. The court appointed attorney didn't even get me a reasonable bail. That didn't matter because thanks to Trina and Dale, I had a new lawyer. Ms. Monroe didn't want to divulge that China refused to pay her, but I'd figured it out. In jail, you have nothing but time on your hands. I analyzed it so much that it was clear what China was doing. I didn't have proof she set me up, but I did know she refused to pay for an attorney for me and that was unforgiveable.

Dale decided to use some of Tony's money without me even having to ask. He felt guilty for Tony leaving me out there struggling, which led me to do what I did in the first place.

I laughed out loud, wishing I could have seen China's face when they hauled her off to jail. She probably thought she was home free. Thought I wouldn't snitch. Ain't no loyalty in these streets especially when dealing with a ratchet like China. She thought she could outsmart all of us, but she couldn't. After my new lawyer, Ms. Monroe, got him to agree to our terms, I sang like a canary when Agent Marks asked me questions.

I kept Trina's name out of it. She had three kids. No need in those kids suffering for something we'd done. Trina was the only one on the outside I could depend on. I couldn't depend on my so-called husband, and I sure couldn't depend on China.

The next few days I fell into a routine. I showered when commanded to do so, ate at the hours designated, and the rest of the time I spent in my cell doing nothing.

One of the prison guards knocked. "Told you to enjoy it while you could. You got a roommate."

I sat up in the bed. Came face to face with my frenemy.

SWIPE

CHINA

The judge refused to give me bail and stuck me in this hell hole. Being in here was bad enough, but did they have to stick me in the cell with Mia?

The guard practically shoved me in the cell. I gave her a look.

"You two get acquainted. This will be your home for a while." The guard laughed and left us alone.

"What's up?" I said, unsure of what else to say. I didn't know how much she knew.

Mia shifted on her bunk and scooted all the way to the back. Her legs dangled over the mattress. "Bet you didn't expect to be joining me, now did you?"

I shrugged. "If I got to be locked up, at least it's with a friend."

"Bitch, you're no friend of mine."

The line had been drawn. There was no way I was staying in the cell with Mia. I turned around and yelled out, "Guard!"

"Lights out," Mia said as she grabbed me around the neck.

Something sharp pricked my neck and blood shot out. I opened my mouth to scream, but nothing came out. I felt my body falling and faded to black.

- THE END -

KAYENNE

READING GROUP
DISCUSSION QUESTIONS

1. Why did Trina go along with the plan? Should she have reconsidered since she had kids to think about?

2. Do you think Mia was justified about her initial feelings concerning China? Why or why not?

3. Did China think she was better than her two friends? If so, give an example.

4. Do you think the friendship between the three ladies was genuine? Give an example to support your answer.

5. How often do you think identity theft occurs in real life?

6. What are some ways you can protect yourself from becoming a victim?

7. What did you think about the men in the book?

8. Why do you think Mia wanted to protect Trina?

9. Would you have trusted China? Trina? Mia?

10. In the end, do you feel like they each got what they deserved?

SWIPE

KAYENNE

BIO

Louisiana writer Kayenne, pronounced just like the pepper Cayenne, likes to write stories with passion. Kayenne's ever-growing legion of fans know her for always adding that *spicy sizzle* to urban lit that keeps them coming back. She loves to hear from readers. Her email is kayennewrites@aol.com or like her page on :

Facebook:
www.facebook.com/KayenneTheAuthor
Twitter: www.twitter.com/Kayennewrites

SWIPE

Butterfly

A NOVEL BY

Michael A. Robinson

WAHIDA CLARK PRESENTS
VENOM IN MY VEINZ
A NOVEL BY
RUMONT TEKAY
ON SALE NOW
FOLLOW RUMONT TEKAY ON ALL SOCIAL MEDIA
// AVAILABLE NOW // ON ITUNES / NOOK / KINDLE / AUDIBLE//
W W W . W C L A R K P U B L I S H I N G . C O M

WAHIDA CLARK PRESENTS
GAME OF GWOP
A NOVEL BY
TRAE MACKLIN
ON SALE NOW!
WWW.WCLARKPUBLISHING.COM // ITUNES | NOOK | KINDLE | AUDIBLE